Also by Susanna Shore

Two-Natured London series

House of Magic

Tracy Hayes, P.I. with the Eye

P.I. Tracy Hayes 4

Susanna Shore

Crimson House Books

Book Design: A. K. S. Keinänen
Cover Design: A. K. S. Keinänen

ISBN 978-952-7061-26-8 (paperback edition)
ISBN 978-952-7061-25-1 (e-book edition)

www.susannashore.com

Chapter One

I WAS TRYING TO KEEP A TRAY-FULL of champagne flutes from gliding to the floor when the thief struck. I was serving Mrs. Snobby-as-fuck at the time, and contemplating her impressive, jewel-adorned cleavage with fascinated horror. I was kind of hoping one of the milling guests at the upscale party would nudge me from behind, so that I could "accidentally" douse her with champagne—or the sparkling white wine the glasses actually contained, about which she'd been complaining to me for the past five minutes. But no one bumped into me.

I was sorely tempted to soak her anyway.

It wasn't just her complaining that irritated me, or the fact that her dress, which she was too old and portly to wear, probably cost more than I made in a year. It wasn't even that it was the night before Thanksgiving and I should've been at my parents' house helping Mom prepare for it instead of serving simulacrum champagne and hors d'oeuvres to the who's who of Brooklyn—and probably half of Manhattan as well.

No, it was the misery of being back to waitressing after three months as a private detective. And worse yet, my body had naturally activated the muscles needed to hold the large trays for hours on end while wearing high heels. I had been waitress extraordinaire once, and it was as if I'd never stopped. Even my attitude became subdued as befit a person in a servile position.

Not exactly my natural state.

The only thing that saved Mrs. I-know-champagne-when-I-taste-it from getting a bubbly white bath was the knowledge that this was only a temporary assignment. I wasn't back to waitressing for good. I was undercover for a case. I couldn't mess this up or my boss would be very upset. And when Jackson Dean, my boss at Jackson Dean Investigations, became upset, he got angry. Then he would yell at me, which would upset me.

It wasn't so much the yelling that did it—he was entertaining to watch—but the knowledge that I'd earned his anger. I'd been on a roll this past month and preferred to continue my winning streak. He'd only yelled at me, like, once or maybe twice, if you counted the time I slept in and forgot to show up for our morning jog. He'd run two and a half miles from his home in Marine Park to Midwood where I lived, in rain, just to vent his aggravation to me.

That's dedication.

"What is your name, girl?" Mrs. Real-champagne-has-tinier-bubbles demanded in a haughty tone you didn't often hear outside British period dramas.

"Jessica, ma'am."

It wasn't. My name's Tracy Hayes, but I wasn't going to tell her that. I was undercover, after all. However, why I gave her the name of my former roommate eluded me. Especially since it wasn't the name I'd picked for this job. I'd chosen Henrietta Fern, for those curious, a name that had caused Jackson infinite mirth. His undercover name was Dean Jones, which totally lacked imagination in my opinion, but which he'd said was easy to remember in a tight spot. I guess he was right.

Don't tell him I said that.

Jessica and I had parted on nasty terms about a month ago when she'd moved away with some of my furniture without asking my permission. I'd retaliated by confronting her in front of her date, one Thomas Thane Westley, a tech start-up millionaire and—incidentally—the host of the party tonight.

He hadn't remembered me when he briefed Jackson and me about the evening, and Jessica was no longer his girlfriend, so I hadn't had to face her here. But perhaps I'd been subconsciously bracing for the encounter and the name just popped out.

"Well, *Jessica*, why don't you scurry into the kitchen and bring me proper champagne," Mrs. I'm-too-important-to-be-served-inferior-stuff suggested with an arrogant sneer. I widened my professional smile from polite to indulgent, as if it were my privilege to serve her, and said, "Right away," without the least intention of doing so, and turned to leave.

That's when the fire alarm went off.

The entire roomful of people froze when the loud beeping started. The large loft apartment had an open floor plan—only the kitchen at the back and the bedrooms on the mezzanine were closed off—and the sound echoed from the high ceiling and bare redbrick walls, making it impossible to detect where it came from.

"Is that the fire alarm?" the woman demanded, affronted, as if it was a personal insult to her.

"I'll go investigate." I pushed the tray at her and she instinctively accepted it. Then I dashed off as fast as I could in my high-heels, ignoring her protests.

I located Jackson in the foyer at the foot of the curving metal and glass stairs leading up. I'd forgotten he was wearing a suit tonight, so it took me a moment to spot him, as I kept looking for a man in a black tee and jeans. I barely recognized him in his James Bond getup and I startled when my eyes landed on him. He looked good.

Don't tell him I said that either.

"What's going on?" I asked, raising my voice to be heard over the noise.

"Fucked if I know. I've been keeping an eye on these stairs the whole evening. No one's gone up, so it can't be the safe's alarm."

The reason we were undercover was to protect the host from being burglarized. There had been a series of break-ins at the finest homes in New York the past month, mostly on Manhattan and always during a party like this one. While the house was filled with people and the hosts busy, the thief snuck in, broke into the house safe, and left with whatever they contained. The police had no clues.

Thomas Thane Westley hadn't wanted to take chances. "I don't have valuables in my safe, but I do keep some important papers there." Since he didn't want to ruin his first big party after listing his company by bringing in the cops, he'd selected us. The police assumed the thief either impersonated a guest or was someone from the upper echelons of society to get an invitation, so we were here to keep an eye on the guests.

"I doubt I'll be targeted, since the thief seems to know when there are valuables in the house, but better safe than sorry."

It seemed Mr. Westley had been wrong. And that spelled trouble for us if we couldn't handle the situation.

The irritating beeping continued without anyone seeming to be able to do anything about it. "I think it's the fire alarm," I said to Jackson, who nodded, sweeping his gaze over the guests, who were looking at each other uncertainly, wondering if the situation was serious enough to merit evacuation and leaving a perfectly good party.

"But what caused it? And is it genuine?"

"I'll go check the kitchen," I said, assuming that if there was a fire, the kitchen was the likeliest source.

I'd barely taken a step towards the other end of the room where the kitchen was when there was a sort of "whoosh" sound and the sprinklers began spewing cold water on us. It cut off the beeping, so I took it as an improvement. Not so the others.

Screams and curses filled the air, and the guests began milling towards the front door, their heads pressed down and hands over their heads to protect their fine hairdos, as if it would help against the determination of the finest sprinkler system money could buy. In mere moments, everyone and everything was drenched and the floor was swimming.

Jackson took instant charge. He was a former cop, so he was trained for it, and he was the kind of person who naturally assumed he was the one you should listen to when things went apeshit. He rushed to open the door out of the apartment and began to issue orders about exiting in an orderly fashion and not to use the elevator. I don't think anyone paid any attention. They were in too much of a hurry to get out of the cold water raining down.

I wanted to flee too. I didn't have a death wish, and a house fire was one of my least favorite ways to die. But I didn't see or smell any smoke, and since I was wet anyway, I couldn't get more miserable than I already was. My clothes weren't expensive and a couple of drops of water wouldn't ruin them.

I retreated a few steps up the stairs to get out of the way of the people pushing towards the door. Water was dripping down my face and into my eyes, but from my higher vantage point I got a good look at how Brooklyn's finest treated each other in a crisis situation. It was pretty ugly. I wouldn't trust any of them to have my back. There wasn't a woman so old or so feeble that she wouldn't be pushed out of the way by a strong younger man. I was about to dash over to one such woman when she bashed one such man with her handbag. She clearly didn't need any help from me.

The crowd was thinning, but not very fast—the door wasn't wide enough for their disorderly exit. But they were consistently pushing to the same direction.

All but one man. He was calmly heading to the kitchen as if he didn't even notice the chaos around him.

Now, he could've been a man blessed with more than common sense, who had realized that the place had to have a second exit through the kitchen that no one else was taking. But there was something in his studied nonchalance that instantly put my Spidey senses on alert. Or whatever senses private detectives have.

I considered my course of action for as long as it took me to slip off my high heels. Then I pushed into the exiting throng, as heedless of their well-being as they were of each other's. I'm average height, and half the Brooklyn Nets seemed to be among the guests, judging by how they towered over me, but what I lacked in vertical reach, I more than made up for with the sharpness of my elbows. They met their targets unerringly, and in no time at all I was through the milling people. The floor clear before me, I took off at full speed—or as fast as I was able to through the water—after the man who had already disappeared into the kitchen.

Behind me, the first shouts erupted:

"My necklace!"

"My wallet."

And then the inevitable: "Did that girl take them?"

"Stop that girl!"

But I couldn't pause to tell them they had the wrong person, because I now knew I had the right one. Sliding on the wet hardwood floor, I pushed through the swinging doors into the kitchen, only to see the man exit through the open back door.

Chapter Two

"HALT!" I SHOUTED, A BIT BREATHLESS, not sure if it was wise to alert the man to my pursuit, but hoping he would obey so that I wouldn't have to continue chasing him.

That didn't happen.

He shot down the back stairs and I did my best Bambi-on-ice impression running after him over the slippery tile floor, bumping against the kitchen island and hurting my hip in the process. I didn't let that slow me down and was soon at the stairs too, taking them down as fast as I could. At least the sprinklers weren't spewing water there, so it was safer going. I could see him two floors down already, an impossible head start in a normal situation, but I was pumped up on adrenaline and determination, and I knew I would catch him.

That didn't happen either—but I came really close. The service entrance was locked and the man had to pause to switch the two handles designed to piss off a harried housekeeper with her hands full trying to get through. He only had one hand free; the other held a black velvet pouch that I assumed contained his ill-gained goods. He fumbled with the lock, giving me a chance to reach the ground floor too.

"This is the police!" I shouted, totally untruthfully—and illegally—but he was a thief and I didn't think a small lie would be such a big deal. Only it was.

The man abandoned the door for long enough to turn sharply around and pitch the pouch in his hand at me like he was on the mound in the middle of the Yankee Stadium. It felt like a baseball too when it hit me in the face, dropping me like a fly.

The next thing I knew was Jackson's blurry face hovering above me. "Tracy! Talk to me. Are you all right?"

"Goffmyface," I slurred, pushing his chest for further measure, but neither had any impact on him.

"What happened?"

I blinked until his face sharpened. It was a nice face, clean-lined and manly, but fascinatingly unnoticeable when he wanted it to be. It was crowned with slightly overgrown dark brown hair—now wet and plastered around his face like he was modelling for the cover of a Regency romance—and brown eyes that could see through your bullshit when he wanted the truth out of you. Currently they were worried, the little lines around them softened.

"You have a nice face," I stated. He shook his head,

but a small smile lifted the corner of his mouth.

"You have a concussion. I have to get you to the hospital."

"No, you have to run after the thief," I remembered, trying to get up, but a dizzy spell made spots dance in my eyes, so I changed direction and lay down instead.

"What? Who? Is that why you took off like that?"

"Yes." I thought it was plenty of information, but the down-tilt of his straight dark brows indicated otherwise. "I saw a man who headed calmly to the kitchen instead of rushing to the front door in a panic, and got suspicious. When I ran after him, he fled, confirming my suspicions." Honest men didn't flee; that was a cop fact. "I almost caught him too, but then he threw his loot at my face." I turned my head in both directions, but the floor was empty. Figured he'd taken time to fetch it back. Had he even checked if I was all right?

Jackson's frown deepened to scary, but for once it wasn't directed at me. He probed my face with gentle fingers, and I winced in pain when he hit the good spot on my temple.

"Nose isn't broken at least, but you'll have a black eye tomorrow," he declared. He felt the back of my head. "There's a bump here you probably got when you fainted."

"I did not faint," I said indignantly. "I was knocked out."

"Even worse. The police are on their way. Can you get up? You have to talk to them before we go to the hospital."

"Aren't you running after the thief?"

"It took me almost five minutes to get here. He's long gone."

Five minutes was a long time to be unconscious, but with Jackson's help I managed to get up, mostly because I'd started to feel cold on the tile floor in my wet clothes and didn't want to lie there anymore. I felt slightly nauseated, but at least not like I needed to throw up. His arm around my waist holding me up, Jackson walked me into the huge service elevator at the end of the hallway, propped me against its wall, and pushed the button to the top floor.

"I thought you said no elevators."

"There was no fire, so they're safe to use."

It was a slow ride up the five floors in the steady service elevator, but still faster than walking in my current state. My head hurt, my face ached, and I shivered all over in the wet clothes that were clinging to my body. Jackson's clothes hugged his body too, but the wet-dress-shirt look was made for his wide shoulders and tight abs that pushed against the fine, white—wet— cotton.

"Sexy..." I drawled, only realizing I'd said it aloud when he rolled his eyes, amused.

"The sooner we get your head scanned the better."

"It's hardly a sign of a brain damage if a girl appreciates a fine body," I said defensively as I followed him out of the elevator, without his support this time.

"With you, it definitely is," he countered.

"I'm perfectly capable of admiring male assets without a concussion." I was too, though occasionally my reaction to them caused me to behave as if I had hit my head.

"I've seen it. Just not mine."

"Maybe I would if you dressed like this all the time and not in endless black T-shirts."

"I'll stick to black, thanks," he said dryly, leading me to the kitchen, where trays of perfectly good food and adequate sparkling white wine stood ruined by the water that had mercifully stopped falling. I gave them a mournful look as I followed Jackson to the main living area. I'd had my heart set on some of those little nibbles.

The main area hadn't fared any better than the kitchen, but it was nothing money couldn't replace, and Thomas Thane Westley had plenty of that. The beautiful hardwood floors would be lost though, if someone didn't dry them as soon as possible. But since it wasn't my problem, I just waded through the ankle-deep water to the man himself, a passable-looking guy in his late thirties, in an expensive—now ruined—suit. He was standing in the middle of the seating area, talking to two plainclothes detectives. Most of the guests had left, but a few of them had remained, probably those who had had their property stolen, judging by their reaction when they spotted me.

"There she is! Arrest her," the horrible woman I'd been talking to when this started demanded with a loud voice. The jewels that had filled her cleavage were gone. The cops turned to me and grinned.

"If it isn't the little apprentice P.I.," one of them said, as if we knew each other well, even though I couldn't even remember his name. He was, however, one of the cops from the 78th Precinct that was a block from our agency, and we often had our lunches in the same place near it. I knew all their faces. "What did you do this time?"

"I almost caught the thief," I declared proudly.

"Almost doesn't count in this business," the other cop said—Pete something or other.

"It's still closer than you've got. And I would've caught him too, if the bastard hadn't thrown his loot at my face."

This got their attention. "You have his description?"

"I do indeed."

"You'll have to come to the station and look through some photos," Pete said, and I was about to agree when Jackson interfered.

"She was unconscious for more than five minutes.

She has to go to the hospital first. She'll look at them after the holidays."

I saw nothing wrong with his plan, but the annoying woman inhaled audibly. "That is unacceptable. I demand you arrest this young woman immediately. She's probably in league with the thief. She wouldn't even serve me proper champagne!"

"Hey! This isn't my party. I'm not responsible for the beverages. Blame him," I said, miffed, pointing at Thomas Thane Westley. An indignant flush rose to his face.

"I'll have you know it was the finest American sparkling wine," he stated. But the woman would have none of that.

"I am not accustomed to drinking anything but champagne."

"I'm not serving imported stuff when there's a perfectly good domestic option available," Westley declared, his voice trembling with patriotism I was pretty sure was faked, and so was the woman.

"You're an upstart with no taste, and cheap to boot. Now, I demand to know, what are you going to do to recover my necklace?"

"This isn't a time-sensitive case," Pete said calmly. "We'll look through the security footage and Miss Hayes will give her statement once the doctor releases her." He put an emphasis on *doctor*, but it didn't really mollify her.

"It was my grandmother's emerald necklace! I cannot have it stay in the hands of some common thief."

"Be that as may, we need to go to hospital," Jackson said, and without waiting for an answer, took me by my arm and led me away.

An hour later I was lying on my back in the CT-scanner.

Chapter Three

J ACKSON DIDN'T HAVE SPECIAL INSURANCE for me that would get me past the ER lines, though he claimed his premiums had skyrocketed since I started working for him. That was hardly my fault—I'd only been shot that one time. It had been a shallow flesh wound too, nothing to write home about.

No, the reason I got a fast-lane treatment was my sister Theresa—Tessa for short—who worked as an ER doctor at the University Hospital of Brooklyn, where Jackson had taken me. Tessa was six years older than me and an overachiever, so we didn't have much in common, but when it came to taking care of the family, she was solid. In short order she had examined my face, which she declared wasn't broken but would bruise badly, and then whisked me off to have my head scanned.

I wished I'd had a chance to pee before I was put in the machine. It was difficult to relax when your bladder demanded your attention.

In due order I was released from the machine, had

answered the call of nature, and sat in front of Tessa, who had taken a look at my scans. Her face was inscrutable, but it always was. For a woman with such a perfectly beautiful face, she seldom expressed anything with it. I used to envy her looks and her naturally auburn hair—currently cut in short pixie style—but I'd sort of grown out of it. I'd even stopped dyeing my mousy brown hair auburn after I'd discovered a hairdresser who could dye it a delicious cherry red.

Well, it was currently sort of cotton candy pink—though not as fluffy thanks to the sprinklers—because the cherry red had faded and I hadn't had money to have it dyed again. I liked this color too, but it wasn't very inconspicuous, which made surveillance work a tad difficult. Luckily we hadn't had any cases recently that required it.

However, I did envy Tessa's long and slim legs that she crossed before propping her elbow against her desk. She was half a head taller than me with a supermodel body—literally—she'd inherited from Dad, whereas my more Mother-Earthly body came from Mom.

"There is slight swelling in your brain," she declared, but from her tone I couldn't detect if it was life-threatening or not, so I opted for humor.

"More to think with, then."

"It doesn't work that way, you know."

I did know that, but it was no use to tell her that. She

completely lacked the humor gene, which for offspring of two Irish people was odd.

"You'll have to take it easy for at least a couple of days. No heavy lifting, no running, and no operating any complicated machinery, including cars. And don't stay alone tonight. Go to Mom's and tell her to keep an eye on you tonight."

"Why?" Mother wasn't exactly old and feeble, and she was a nurse to boot, but I needed a good reason to keep her awake the night before Thanksgiving.

"People with concussions can asphyxiate during sleep," she stated, with the same tone she might say "milk is white". Much like my face was, after all the blood fled to my feet.

"You mean I could die of this?"

"Of course. Hits to the head are always serious." Then, as if she hadn't just delivered horrible news, she relaxed a little. "Are you going to Mom and Dad's for Thanksgiving?"

The change of topic fazed me, especially since my lethally swollen brain was slow to compute. "Of course." Where else would I go? I was single, divorced with no children, and even my roommate wouldn't be home. But since she knew it, I didn't ask it aloud.

"Do you think I could bring Angela?"

Tessa had stunned all of us—well, those of us who knew about it—by starting to date a woman. We'd kept our parents in the dark though, and I wasn't sure their reaction would be positive. But I shrugged. "Sure. Mom's already upset that Travis is taking Melissa and the kids to Melissa's parents this year. Might as well add your news to the pile."

She flashed me a genuine smile that both transformed her face to impossibly more beautiful and made her look much like Dad. "Great. We'll see you tomorrow, then."

And so unsettled was I by her news that I forgot to worry about my impending death. Instead I churned over all the possible scenarios of how Thanksgiving dinner could go wrong, until Jackson pulled over outside my parents' house in Kensington.

"Do you have plans for tomorrow?" I asked.

He shrugged. "Not really. Emily travelled to see her family, so I thought I'd just order in some pizza and watch the game."

I'd mostly asked to have him as a buffer at dinner, but the sad image softened my heart. He was an only child and his parents were dead. He had nowhere to go. And no one should be alone on Thanksgiving.

"Then you'll come to have dinner with us," I declared.

"I will?" he asked, but I could see he was secretly pleased I'd invited him. I would've done it earlier, but I'd thought he had made plans with his girlfriend of the past two months.

"Yes. Mom would love to have you, and there's plenty of room now that Travis's family won't be there."

"In that case, thank you for the invitation. Can I bring anything?"

"Can you cook?"

"Not really," he admitted with a grin. I smiled too.

"Just bring your appetite. Mom always makes plenty."

"I remember. This won't be the first Thanksgiving I'm spending with your family." He'd been friends with my eight-years-older brother Travis when they were kids. His family hadn't exactly been nurturing, so he'd spent a lot of time in our house. Not that I remembered him; the house had been lousy with boys when I was little, and I'd tried to avoid them the best I could.

"I'll see you tomorrow, then." With a wave of my hand I exited the car and slipped into the house, hoping not to wake up Mom.

No such luck.

That was why mid-morning found me in the nearby playground, sitting at the edge of a sandbox, making choo-choo sounds with a plastic bulldozer. I knew they didn't make that noise, I just couldn't figure out what kind of sound they should make. Besides, my charge didn't care about the accuracy of engine noises; he was too busy building a castle my bulldozer could destroy.

Mom had had a fit when I came home, as if as a wife

and mother of cops she wasn't used to little work-related accidents like mine. And when in the morning my face indeed turned out to be interestingly bruised, black and blue bleeding from my temple around my right eye, she had declared I would have to take the morning easy.

Since I wasn't much of a household goddess, she was probably relieved I wasn't in the kitchen messing up her careful dinner preparations. But why she thought it would be a good option to send me to the park with my nephew, Mason, I had no idea. It involved everything Doctor Tessa said I shouldn't do: running and heavy lifting, and I'm fairly sure looking after a three-year-old constituted as operating complicated machinery too. At least his questions tasked my brain excessively.

"Why is this leaf brown and this leaf red, Aunt Tracy?" he asked, pushing the leaves to my face as if I couldn't perfectly well see them farther away.

"I don't know, sweetie. Maybe the other one is dressed in the last season's fashion."

"Where have all the worms gone, Aunt Tracy?"

"To Florida for the holidays."

I was proud of my answers, and since the little tyke accepted them without arguments, I felt like I'd done a good job. But the other mothers on the playground shot me reproachful glances and pulled their children away from my dumbing influence. Or it could be my face that caused it. I'd used a ton of makeup, sunglasses, and a large hat to conceal the bruise, but you could still detect a glimpse if you paid attention. I could hear them muttering about bad mothers and whether they should contact Child Protective Services.

Good luck with that.

There was nothing wrong with little Mason's home conditions, if you didn't count the fact that his mother had dumped him on his unsuspecting father and left for Africa for two months to take care of an Ebola outbreak for Doctors Without Borders. She'd just shown up on Halloween with the cutest little boy you could imagine— all curly orange hair, dimply knees, and chubby cheeks— and pretty much forced the issue, because she had no one else who could look after him. A caring mother would probably have checked with the father first before signing the contract.

Trevor, my four-years-older brother, and the father in question, could be trusted to look after his son perfectly. He might not know anything about children, but he was a cop and very reliable. It was just that he hadn't known he had a son and it had taken him these past couple of weeks to get over the shock. He'd hooked up with the ambitious doctor for one night and hadn't expected to hear from her again—and definitely not like this. But since the boy was his spitting image at the same age, it was difficult to question his provenance. He had made an effort to learn to know his son and how to look after him, but he was a homicide detective and his hours weren't exactly nine to five, which made it difficult for him to be there for Mason when he needed him—which, for the first couple of days, had been constantly, as the poor kid missed his mom.

The rest of us had stepped in. My parents had been over the moon about the new grandchild—after having gotten over the out-of-wedlock thing. Dad especially had risen to the occasion, which was made easier because Trevor still lived with our parents. Dad was a retired cop and bored out of his mind. There was nothing he loved more than looking after Mason to fill his days, kicking a small ball in the tiny backyard and teaching him how to hammer nails into a block of wood for days on end.

Even I had taken a few babysitting duties. It couldn't be said I thrived at it, but so far the child hadn't met any serious injury in my care and that was something. And I intended to keep it that way.

Chapter Four

"C UTE KID," SAID A RASPY VOICE from the other side of the sandbox of a woman who'd spent her young life smoking everything illegal. She was thin, and looked much older than her twenty something years would indicate, but her hair and clothes were clean. Her child about Mason's age looked fairly well-fed and was playing happily with a sand scoop.

I looked around. The playground had emptied of the well-to-do mothers while I hadn't paid attention. Kensington, the neighborhood where my childhood home was, a street after a long street of detached clapboard houses with tiny yards, was fast being gentrified. The working class families like mine were being replaced by lawyers and bankers and such, evident even on the playground in the high-tech prams and expensive toys the mothers boasted. But the edges were still tenements for those with a tenuous grip on life, and now the playground was furtively being filled with mothers who hadn't had quite as good starts to their lives but who were doing their damnedest to see that their children would have better childhoods.

"Thanks, yours too." And I wasn't even lying.

"Your old man did that?"

It took me a moment to understand what she was asking, and then my hand lifted self-consciously to my face. It wasn't as sore as the bruise would indicate. "No, I'm not married."

The woman gave a throaty laugh. "What does marriage have to do with getting beaten up?"

I had to smile too. "No, I mean it wasn't a domestic thing. Or even an accident. But you're right, it was deliberate."

"Oh?"

"I'm a private detective and I tried to arrest someone. It didn't go as I hoped it would."

"Occupational hazard?"

"With me anyway."

She laughed again and we settled to watch the children move sand from one pile to another. It didn't occupy my whole attention though. Like I'd watched the other mothers earlier, I watched the new women in the park interacting with their children. Call it professional curiosity, and not just because I was a P.I.; I'd done the same when I was waitressing. People interested me.

Much was the same as with the richer moms, if you ignored the material discrepancy: a keen eye was kept on the offspring and boo-boos were handled with TLC.

But unlike the earlier mothers, these mothers weren't as social. No clusters formed to spend the outdoors hour gossiping, exchanging the latest theories in child-rearing, or talking about the best preschools. And at the edge of the park, on a lone bench, sat a hunched form of a woman who didn't seem to have a child to look after at all. She just kept chain-smoking and staring into her thoughts. My curiosity piqued, I addressed the woman who had spoken earlier.

"What's her story?" I asked, nodding at the lone woman. Tears shot to my companion's eyes, and she pulled her child closer.

"Her baby boy has disappeared, maybe kidnapped."

My heart stopped, only to resume beating at a much faster pace, and I sat closer to Mason. "How? When?"

"She was returning from this park last month and paused to buy cigarettes. When she turned around the kid was gone."

"What did the police say?"

"Nothing. They have 'no clues,' as if they'd even looked properly," the woman said, her voice bitter. I wanted to protest on principle, but I knew people like the women in this park tended not to be a high priority for the police. But surely a child disappearing would get some attention, no matter who the parents were? I'd have to ask Trevor.

Another woman spoke, a timid-looking creature who I

would've thought would be too afraid to say anything in public. "That's not even the only child who's disappeared lately. I heard Trixie's cousin's ex's child was taken too."

"From this same park?" I asked, horrified. I wouldn't bring Mason here again, if that was the case.

"No, the one near the school."

Still, too close to home. Feeling less happy than a moment ago, I thanked the women and wished them happy Thanksgiving. Then I put Mason into his stroller, much to his protests, and hurried home.

Mom had dinner preparations well underway, and since Dad took charge of Mason, it freed me to help her. Lots of peeling was involved, even though I tried to tell her I couldn't be trusted around sharp objects.

"You look fine," Mom said. She hadn't turned sixty yet, and though she was softer and rounder than in her youth, she still had a spring in her step and there was no gray in her strawberry-blond hair. I took after her in looks and shape—round in the round bits, with a tendency to fill up, and not overly tall—but not in coloring. "Park did you good."

"I'm not sure about that." I told her what I'd learned and her face set in grim lines.

"I heard about a similar incident at the clinic not long ago." Mom worked at a nearby maternity clinic that offered free medical services once a week for mothers who couldn't afford other places.

"And the police aren't doing anything?"

"I'm sure they are." Mom's trust in them was unwavering after almost forty years as a cop's wife.

"Well, I'm not. I'll have to talk with Trevor."

That would have to wait though, as he was working most of the day and would only return in time for dinner. We would eat early, a remnant from when we were kids, and important again now that there were little ones attending. Though it was only Mason this year, which Mom didn't stop sighing about the whole time we prepared dinner.

"Melissa's parents have every right to have their grandchildren with them on Thanksgiving," I tried to say, but to no avail.

"Both her sisters have children too. Aren't those enough?"

"At least this frees us up to pay more attention to Mason."

Secretly I was glad that Travis's four-year-old twins Brandon and Chad weren't attending. They were cute and all, but a handful. Or two handfuls, as it were. I called them Damien 1 and 2 after the demon kid in Omen, a movie I shouldn't have watched when I was only seven, but I'd snuck into the living room one evening when Travis was watching it with his friends. Only my frightened cry during a scary scene had revealed my hiding place and then I'd been driven away. To this day I didn't know how the movie ended, and I wasn't sure if it was worse than if I did.

"And when are you going to give me grandchildren already?" Mom asked, taking me by surprise. Not that she didn't often ask it.

"In or out of wedlock?"

"Not funny, Tracy."

"The latter is currently the only option I have." And even that wasn't really an option, because I hadn't dated anyone in years. I'd sworn off men after witnessing my husband—now resolutely ex-husband—cheating on me. It had been six years ago, but I'd yet to start dating again. First there hadn't been time, as I'd been working constantly, and now that my hours were more flexible I hadn't met anyone who interested me enough to try.

"You're twenty-seven already."

"I know, Mom."

"You should've let me fix you up with that doctor from the clinic."

"We've been over this already. You know our tastes in men don't align."

"What's wrong with your father?"

I blinked at the question. "Nothing. But you've never tried to fix me up with someone like him."

She sighed. "That's because I know how hard it is to be married to a cop."

"I'll take a cop over a doctor any day."

"I'll keep that in mind." She would too.

I was saved by the doorbell announcing Jackson's arrival. He was back in his customary black, though he wore a nice cashmere sweater instead of a T-shirt, which looked really good on him. I'd forgotten to tell Mom about inviting him, but she didn't bat an eye and welcomed him with great delight. Behind his back she raised her brows at me knowingly, but I shook my head. He wasn't my boyfriend or anything.

"I brought this," he said, giving a huge bowl of salad to Mom, who accepted it with a smile and disappeared into the kitchen with it.

"I thought you said you can't cook," I said to him.

"I could make a salad if I had to, but that's not mine. Cheryl showed up early this morning with it. She wanted to make sure I had something homemade this Thanksgiving."

"That was nice of her." Cheryl was the agency's secretary whom Jackson had inherited along with the agency from his uncle. She was spending the weekend with her daughter's family on the west side of the state border, i.e. New Jersey.

"Salad's not all she gave me." He grimaced. "She couldn't take Misty with her, and I couldn't leave her alone all day, so I brought her with me. Is that okay?"

"Did you leave her in the car?" I headed to the door to rescue the poor thing. Misty Morning was Cheryl's border terrier Yorkie mix we'd gotten her a while back during a case, a small black and brown thing that loved everyone. Including me, as evidenced by the delighted barking that greeted me when I opened the door.

"No, on the porch," Jackson said with a grin, watching the dog try to wash my face as if she hadn't seen me in ages, when I kneeled to scratch her.

"Ouch, stop that," I admonished her when her nose hit my bruise.

"Does your face hurt?" Jackson asked, instantly worried, studying the evidence of my failure. I got up holding the dog.

"Not terribly, unless someone pokes at it." I carried Misty to the living room, where Dad and Mason were watching TV. The dog was an instant hit among the three-year-olds of the house. Dad had more reservations.

"Trevor's allergic to dogs. What if Mason is too?" He was in his early sixties and tall, if not quite as straight-backed as in his youth. His black Irish hair was turning gray, but the blue of his eyes was still sharp.

"Only one way to find out." We kept a keen eye on the little boy, but when he didn't instantly start wheezing, we relaxed and let the two of them play. I smiled. "See, nothing to worry about."

The front door opened and Tessa entered, Angela in tow.

Chapter Five

"**S**HIT," I MUTTERED TO MYSELF, but Jackson heard.

"You didn't expect them?"

"I did. I just forgot to tell my parents about it."

I rushed to the door. Angela was about Tessa's age, with strong Mediterranean features of someone whose family hadn't lived in New York long enough for the lineage to mix. She was half a head shorter than Tessa, and almost equally beautiful, with a curvy body I would kill for, and long black hair currently in a relaxed braid. Of the two, she was more firmly attached to reality. Not that Tessa wasn't perfectly realist. She simply failed to take other peoples' emotions into account.

"Hi, Angela. Welcome," I said warmly, and reached for a hug even though we didn't really know each other well. She was a hugger though, so there was no awkward moment—until I said that my parents didn't know about her. Then she pulled back, her eyes large.

"Shit," she muttered, much like I'd done a moment ago. I introduced Jackson, who had followed me, leaving out the inconvenient fact that he was the P.I. her ex-husband had hired to follow her when he thought she was being unfaithful. And she had been—with my sister, which I'd learned the hard way on that stakeout.

Mom and Dad came to greet her too. They were warm and polite like they always were when meeting our friends, but I feared it would change when they learned the truth. It wasn't my place to tell it though, so I held my tongue when Tessa simply introduced Angela as her friend. Angela didn't protest either.

Angela had brought a traditional Italian pie that smelled delicious. "Tessa told me your family doesn't have ironclad traditions about Thanksgiving food." Then she grimaced. "My ex's mother refused to serve it when I spent Thanksgiving with them the first time."

Mom shook her head, incredulous. "We've always had so many people over that it would've been useless to limit the dishes. This looks wonderful."

Mason came to the foyer carrying Misty awkwardly under her front legs, and presented the dog to Angela. She instantly kneeled to chat with him and scratch the dog, winning both of them over—and probably the rest of the family too. A person who treated children and dogs nicely couldn't be bad.

In due course, we sat down to eat. Trevor arrived only moments before we tucked in. He took after Mom with his strawberry blond hair, green eyes, and stocky, muscled build, though he had some of Dad's height. And even though our colors were different, it was self-evident with a glance that we were related.

It was also evident to everyone that he was having a shitty day, even though he wouldn't say anything and instead sat next to Mason to help him with his plate. But his hand was shaking a little as he cut turkey meat into smaller pieces, so it had to be really bad. I was itching to know what it was, but it would ruin everyone's dinner, so for once I managed to keep my mouth shut.

As was our family tradition, we began dinner by sharing the things we were thankful for this year. Mom and Dad were thankful for the family and their health, and Trevor for Mason. I racked my brain for what I was the most grateful for. My new job had definitely changed my life for the better, even though it could be gruesome.

I settled with, "I'm thankful for my new life and all the people I've come to know because of it," nodding at Jackson, who was sitting next to me. He smiled.

"And I'm thankful that because of you I've re-connected with the wonderful family of my childhood."

That made Mom tear up a little.

"I'm thankful that with Tessa's help, I finally had the strength to leave my husband," Angela said, giving my sister a warm smile. Jackson and I exchanged quick glances, and decided to take at least a bit of credit for that too.

"And I'm grateful that life brought me such a wonderful love who gave me courage to acknowledge who I really am," Tessa said, with an equally warm smile for Angela. I thought it was beautifully said, and more emotionally aware than I would've thought she was capable of, but Mom inhaled sharply.

"What?"

Tessa gave her a calm look, not unlike the one she used with her patients. "Angela isn't just my friend, she's my girlfriend."

Stunned silence fell, mostly because those of us who had known were waiting for the reaction of those who hadn't. Angela was tense.

"Did you know about this, Tracy?" Mom asked with an outraged huff. Definitely not the reaction I'd expected. Back when I'd told my parents I'd married Scott, she'd unleashed the full impact of her ire on me. Of course, it might have been because I'd also announced that I would quit college to follow Scott on tour with his band. My doomsday scenarios for Tessa's announcement had been based on that experience. Apparently I'd been wrong.

"Ummm, yes?"

"And you didn't tell me?"

"It wasn't my place to tell," I tried to defend myself.

"You know perfectly well that your sister isn't good at sharing. You should've come to me immediately."

"How is this my fault all of a sudden?" I asked, offended. I'd done what I thought was right.

Father cleared his throat. Then he cleared it again, struggling for words. "Is this ... permanent?"

"It's not a phase, if that's what you mean," Tessa said, still calm, as if she was oblivious to the turmoil she'd caused. "We've moved in together."

"You're living in sin?" Mom shrieked. "What will I tell Father Seymour?"

Tessa blinked, baffled. "I can marry her, if you think that'll make things better. But Angela's divorced, so I don't think the Church would approve."

"I'm not entirely sure the Church would approve even if she wasn't divorced," I said dryly.

"That's quite enough from you," Mom said sharply, and I crossed my arms over my chest, sulking. Why she would attack me when I'd done nothing was beyond me. Trevor shook his head at me from across the table, clearly asking me to keep my mouth shut. Then he smiled at Angela.

"I for one am glad that you're in Tessa's life. You've managed to make her more human in such a short time."

That was true, but since I wasn't allowed to talk, I continued sulking, even more so when Mom didn't berate him for not telling her. He lived here. He'd had more opportunities for it.

"So, Angela, tell us about yourself," Dad said. He was

clearly still struggling with the news, but at least he was making a civilized effort. Angela gave us the basics. When Mom heard she was a pediatrician, she perked.

"Doctor is quite something, at least. And children's doctors are better than the rest. But what about your children?"

"It's early days for us yet," Tessa said. "But we've agreed that if we want them, Angela will have them."

"So I'll have grandchildren?" Mom asked.

"Yes," Angela said firmly, as if she had already made up her mind. And with that, Mom's mind was at ease—for now. Knowing her, she would seek counselling with Father Seymour. We could only hope the old priest was open-minded.

Crisis averted, we settled to eat the excellent meal with less controversial topics, like: "What happened to your face?" Trevor hadn't been home when I woke up and hadn't heard the story. I abandoned my sulking and gave a vivid account, exaggerating my heroics for a good measure. Jackson grinned, but he didn't contradict me.

"Westley called me this morning and actually thanked us for our swift action," he said.

"Really?" The way these things usually went for me, I got all the blame. "So he'll pay us?"

"Absolutely."

That was good news at least, and I attacked my food with renewed fervor. By the time we'd each had more pie than we could handle, I was so full I couldn't breathe properly. Mason had left the table earlier and was playing happily with Misty in the living room.

"Do you mind putting Mason to bed?" Trevor asked, getting up. "I have to get back to work."

"Is it really necessary?" Dad asked with a frown. "I hoped we could watch the game together."

Trevor's face distorted with pain and sorrow before he managed to control his expression. "We found a dead baby in the park."

My entire being froze. "The Albemarle playground?" That's where I'd been to this morning with Mason.

"No, Prospect." It was a huge park north of Kensington, but not that far from the playground.

"How did the baby die?" Angela asked, full of professional interest.

"We don't know. There are no outward signs of trauma." He took out his phone and opened a photo to show her. She and Tessa studied it with their heads pressed together, their faces impassive, but they wouldn't show it to me, as if I couldn't handle it.

"Could be the baby was shaken too forcibly," Tessa noted.

Okay, maybe I couldn't handle it.

"It's difficult to imagine a parent doing that and then abandoning the body," Trevor said, full of the disbelief of a newly-minted father. We all nodded. He swiped his thumb to another photo, and this time I got a look too, but it was just of the crime scene, an abandoned baby carriage in a gazebo by a lake. Whoever had left it there had meant the body to be found.

"Expensive baby carriage," I said, remembering the conversations from that morning.

"So from a better family," Trevor mused aloud.

"A nanny who lost her temper?" Jackson suggested. Clearly none of us wanted to entertain the idea that a parent would be responsible.

"A parent wouldn't abandon the body. They usually try to pass the death off as an accident," Trevor said, as if reading my thoughts.

"I heard babies have been kidnapped around here," I said, recalling the other conversation from that morning. "What if this was done by the kidnapper? Maybe the baby wouldn't stop crying when they were trying to flee and the kidnapper lost their temper?"

Dismayed faces stared back at me. Trevor shot to action. "I'll check into it. Perhaps the baby was reported kidnapped, so we'll get an ID."

Mason and Misty came to us and Trevor leaned down to give his son a tight hug. Mason wriggled out, clearly perturbed. Then he looked at his dad with large eyes full of wonder. "Did you know that worms move to Florida for holidays?"

"Tracy!"

Chapter Six

J ACKSON HAD PROMISED ME A DAY OFF for Friday, but since I had nothing else to do, I showed up at work at the normal hour anyway, a little before nine. He didn't look surprised, but I'd brought coffee and leftovers of Angela's pie to ensure my welcome. We made a fast job of them.

The turkey sandwiches Mom had made me I stored in the fridge in our office for later, ignoring the soulful looks Misty gave me when she smelled them. She'd eaten more than she should've the previous evening. The fridge already contained the food Mom had given Jackson when he went home after the game ended. That was lunch sorted, then.

Since we had nothing more pressing than the Westley robbery, we headed to the police station so I could give my statement. The agency was located on Flatbush Avenue, a block from Barclays Center, in a fairly upscale location that brought us clientele that could actually afford to pay our fees. Outside, the building looked a bit worn, but the insides were in good repair.

The 78th Precinct was a short block up from Flatbush Avenue, in an elegant limestone building. Most of the patrol cars were gone, probably driving around making sure the Black Friday shopping didn't get out of hand. Inside, it was fairly quiet. We were known there, so the security check was waived, and in a few moments we were sitting in a private meeting room with Detectives Newman—that was Pete—and Migliaccio. I still didn't get his first name.

"Why don't you walk us through the events first," Pete said, leaning forward in his chair, looking eager. He was in his late thirties maybe, and I was pretty sure this was the most high-profile theft he'd had to handle in ages. If it tied to the burglaries, someone higher up would probably take it away from him soon. I was his only shot at cracking the case before that happened.

I gave them my version and they looked suitably impressed with my powers of perception. "And then he beat you up?" Detective Migliaccio asked, appalled.

"No, he threw his loot pouch at my face."

"Good aim, considering he was fleeing," Pete noted, studying the bruise that was still as noticeable as the previous day, even with the makeup. Maybe I should invest in professional grade concealer like makeup artists used. Something told me this wouldn't be my last shiner, and those could hide bruises perfectly.

"He had a good technique too. Like a pro pitcher."

All three men perked. "Could be he'd been one?" Jackson suggested. "There were many sports stars present last night."

"He was no one I recognized."

"And you're an expert on baseball?" Migliaccio sounded so derisive it made my teeth hurt, but I shrugged.

"I have two older brothers and a father who all love it. Difficult not to pick up some things. I haven't watched in recent years, but I doubt he was anyone still playing."

"Why's that?"

"Too old. I'd say late thirties, at least, maybe older."

Migliaccio grimaced. He was older than Newman. I hid my smile.

"And it could be he wasn't a major league player," Jackson reminded us. "Plenty of places for the less famous to play."

"If he even was a former baseball player," Pete said. "Many guys can pitch well, and the distance wasn't that far. If he'd pitched with the force the top players do, I doubt you'd be with us today."

Happy thought.

"So what did he look like?"

I closed my eyes to conjure the image, though I didn't have to. The moment he'd turned around and I saw his face was etched on my retinas. "He was maybe five-ten or eleven, with broad shoulders and a fitted jacket."

"How would you know?" Pete interrupted.

"You don't get a fit that perfect for shoulders that broad off the rack. Anyway, he had short, light brown hair, thinning a little, but it wasn't noticeable unless you got a look from above."

"And you did?"

"Yes, when I followed him down the stairs. Face was unremarkable. At least, I hadn't noticed him among the guests, and I paid good attention to all the men. Lean cheeks, all the bits proportional to each other, eyes not too far or close, nose not too large and no bushy brows. No noticeable features like birthmarks or scars."

"Caucasian?"

"Yes, but well-tanned, like he'd recently returned from a Bahamas vacation."

"This time of year it should make it easier to spot him," Pete noted. "But he doesn't fit any potential suspects we have." He looked annoyed. "Could you talk to our sketch artist so we can get an approximation of what he looks like?"

"Sure." And I did, a curious process where it seemed at first that the two of us didn't understand each other at all, but which in the end produced a passable image of the guy. I shuddered. He hadn't seemed evil, or that desperate even, when he threw the pouch at me. Just perfectly prepared to do whatever it took to escape. And he would do it again, if we crossed paths.

It was time for an early lunch by the time I returned to the office, and Jackson and I shared the leftovers with some diet coke he'd bought. I didn't like the taste, but I endured it because I could use to lose a few pounds. If for nothing else, it would make the mandatory running exercises Jackson had prescribed for me easier.

Misty got some turkey too, and then it was time for her walksies. "Are you game for a longer walk?" I asked Jackson, who cocked an amused brow.

"I am, but is Misty?"

"I can carry her if needed."

"You want to go to Prospect Park," he guessed. When I nodded, he got up. "I think we'll drive there." Since it was a twenty-minute brisk walk just to reach the park, I had nothing against the suggestion.

We didn't take his car that was parked in a garage a couple of blocks from the agency. There was a subway station right outside the building, and a line led straight to the park, so it was far easier to take a train. I carried Misty so she wouldn't get trampled on or stop to show love to every person who walked by. Less than ten minutes after descending underground, we emerged back on the street on the northern edge of the park outside the Brooklyn Museum, a limestone edifice adorned with Greek columns and every single architectural style since.

"Where to now?" I asked Jackson as he led us past

the museum to the park.

"The lake is large, but I think the site has to be at the southern end, because your brother was called in even though the park doesn't belong to his precinct."

"Great. That's two miles, easily."

Jackson grinned. "I thought we came here to walk."

"We could've walked to the 7th Street station and taken the Q to the Parkside Avenue station." That was at the southern end of the park.

"Come on, it'll do you good."

"Can't you at least call Trevor and ask for specifics?"

"Where's the fun in that?"

It was a nice walk, I'll give him that. The day was fine. The botanical garden behind the museum was still pretty with late-blooming roses, and the paths on the other side of Flatbush Avenue that cut through the park were pleasant: part wilderness, part landscaped recreational areas. Misty was a sturdier walker than I'd given her credit for. I was wearing my good sneakers, and Jackson was never out of breath. We kept a brisk pace and reached the southern end of the lake in half an hour. I was enjoying myself greatly.

In the end, we didn't have any trouble finding the crime scene. It was by the main path at the south-eastern corner of Prospect Park Lake, in a large gazebo built of huge peeled logs, and still active. It was cordoned off, watched over by a rookie cop in uniform, and crime scene investigators were combing the area. We watched them work from a distance while Misty quenched her thirst from the lake.

"What exactly did you think to achieve by coming here?" Jackson asked.

"I don't know." I truly didn't. "I just had to see it myself." I told him about the women I'd met the previous day. "I can't help thinking that the police wouldn't be looking this closely if it weren't a child of an affluent family."

"I'm sure the police would do all they could if that other girl's baby had been found dead."

"But they'd be more willing to blame the mother."

Jackson didn't have a comeback for that.

Trevor's black Ford Edge pulled over by the other cars already on the scene, and my brother got out with his partner, Detective Blair Kelley. She was a commanding woman in her early forties who dressed in pantsuits that would've made her clean features and lean body look a bit manly if not for their warm colors. No black, gray or navy for her; it was dark rose, plum, or ruby that made her brown skin glow.

They headed to the cordon, but they just stood there, staring into the gazebo that was now empty of dead babies and their carriers. I doubted either of them really saw it.

We went to them. "Any leads?" Jackson asked without greetings. Those seemed superfluous, or dis-respectful maybe.

Detective Kelley shook her head, looking grim. "None whatsoever. The baby wasn't reported missing or kidnapped anywhere in this state."

"So ... deliberately murdered?" I asked hesitantly. When she nodded, I felt sick.

"What brings you here?" my brother asked.

"We're walking Misty."

A small, tired smile lifted the corner of his mouth. "A long walk for such a small dog."

"She can walk longer than I can."

"I don't doubt it."

"Hey!"

But he just sighed. "There's nothing new, nothing to report. Nothing you can help with."

We'd known that, but it was still upsetting. "You should go home. Have a good sleep. You look like you need it." He didn't answer, and since there truly was nothing we could do here except gawp with the rest of the onlookers, we headed to the nearest subway station and rode back to the agency.

A young man was waiting in the hallway outside our agency door.

Chapter Seven

HIS NAME WAS STEVE CLARK. He was twenty-one and he was a student at Brooklyn College, the same institution of higher learning I'd once attended. Judging by his designer jeans and shirt, he came from some money, but not so much he could've bought himself a place at an ivy-league college.

Or it could be he didn't want to. He struck me as a guy who didn't intend to make any extra effort if less would do. He slouched on the guest chair in front of Jackson's desk as if even holding himself that much upright seemed to task his energies. His hair fell into his face, and not in an artful, designed mess; he simply hadn't bothered to comb it today. There were dark circles under his eyes like he hadn't slept in ages.

"What can we do for you, Mr. Clark?" Jackson asked with his polite tone he used with clients. In a marked contrast to our visitor, he oozed strength and good mood, and I found myself sitting straighter on the couch at the side of the room where I'd made my nest these past three months. Misty was sleeping next to me. She didn't care about our potential client beyond her original greeting.

Steve ran fingers through his unkempt hair. "This can't be made public, or I'll be in trouble at the college." Jackson nodded calmly, but I could see he already didn't respect the boy. "My baby has gone missing."

Jackson and I exchanged stunned looks. I felt sick. "When?" he asked.

"I don't know. Sometime yesterday, maybe."

"Maybe?"

He glanced at me. "He's not mine in anything other than biologically. I only learned he was missing when his mother came to me an hour ago."

"And you came to us instead of the police?" Jackson sounded slightly incredulous, but I doubt the boy noticed.

"She didn't want to go to the police."

"Why not?"

He looked awkward. "She was passed out when the baby disappeared."

That didn't sound like the image I'd had of the mother in my head. Affluent college boys dated affluent college girls, and even if they partied hard and occasionally passed out too, they probably would've had someone to look after the baby.

Jackson clearly thought the same. "Why don't you tell the whole story from the beginning? Who's the mother, how old is the baby, and why aren't you part of the child's life?"

"She was just a hook-up, you know. Not the type I usually go after. A stripper." There went the image I'd had. "There was this party and we had sex, nothing more. Then a couple of months ago she came to me with the baby, so I guess he's three months now, maybe less. She would've contacted me sooner, but it took her a while to track me down."

Props for the girl for resilience. It couldn't have been an easy task to find some drunken frat boy months after meeting him. "She wanted money, of course."

"And did you pay?" Jackson asked, making a note on his pad.

"Of course not. I only had her word that the child was mine."

I blinked. "Then what happened?"

"The bitch contacted my mom and she had a fit. She had no doubt that the baby was mine, but she had him tested, just to be sure. Mine." A disgusted look spread on his face. "But I don't have any money. I won't get any until I turn twenty-five and have the use of what my father left me. I told her that much and she went away."

"Yet she came to you when the baby went missing?"

"Where else could she go? She didn't want to talk to the police 'cause she's afraid that child services will take the baby away from her, so I came to you."

"The police have better resources for these kinds of investigations," Jackson noted, but Steve just shrugged, as if it was the same to him whether or not the baby was found. I could sort of understand that he didn't feel connected to his child, but any child's disappearance should elicit a stronger reaction than this. I fought to not let my anger show while Jackson quoted our prices to him. For a guy with no money, he didn't bat an eye. He just wrote a check for advance expenses, gave us the name and address of the girl, and left.

"That was something else," I said when he was gone. Jackson frowned.

"I don't like this at all. Too many children have gone missing in the same area. I'll call Trevor."

Technically, the disappearances hadn't happened in the jurisdiction of his precinct, but this wasn't a time for technicalities.

"The mother didn't want to involve the police."

"I don't give a fuck what she wants!" Jackson roared.

I'd seldom seen him this angry. Yes, he constantly yelled at me, and mostly for a good reason, but they were light breezes compared to the storm brewing inside him. He surged up, toppling his chair in the process and not even caring. His hands were in such tight fists the larger veins in his arms popped up and I doubt he could've opened them even if he tried. He propped them heavily against the desk.

"Okay, okay, we'll call Trevor," I said in a placating tone as he fought to bring his anger under control. I wondered if this was personal to him, but he hadn't reacted similarly last evening when Trevor showed the pictures of the crime scene, and he'd been relatively calm earlier too when we visited the site.

Misty jumped down from the couch and went to him, circling around his legs and poking his shins with her nose, whining distressed. After a while, Jackson leaned down and picked her up, allowing the dog to work her magic on him.

"Thanks, girl," he said in a tight voice when he put her back down again. He flexed the muscles on his shoulders and neck, bringing himself back in control. "Okay, let's go talk to the mother."

Melody Bell, the mother, lived on McDonald Avenue that formed the western edge of Kensington, near the Albemarle playground where I'd taken Mason the previous day. Hearing the address, I instantly thought of the lone mother smoking on the bench there, but since her child had gone missing a month ago, she couldn't be Melody. Nevertheless, the address was too worrying to be a coincidence.

The area was fast being built full of large, red-brick apartment buildings with their own security and nice yards in front of them, but Melody lived in an older, three-story street-side building that had bars over the windows and retail on the ground floor. An air of neglect hung about the place, as if it was waiting to be demolished.

Contrary to my expectations, the front door wasn't locked. That turned out to be because the lock had been broken some time ago and never fixed. The air inside smelled musty and the floors were gray with dirt, but otherwise it was in relatively good repair. Jackson and I climbed to the second floor up narrow stairs, listening to the sounds of life that came through the walls we were passing. Nothing could remain private in this building.

Melody's door was the last of four on the left of the stairs. Jackson knocked on the doorjamb and we paused to listen, but nothing happened. We couldn't hear any noise from inside the apartment, which gave us a pretty good notion that it was empty. That, or she was holding her breath and not moving.

Jackson knocked again, louder this time. "Melody Bell? Are you home?" He leaned his ear against the door to listen—contrary to all the security measures he'd tried to drill me—and the door opened. "Melody?"

He pushed the door all the way open and we went carefully in. It gave straight into a small room that was clean and sparsely furnished with an open hide-a-bed and a small dining table. On the left was a small recess with a kitchenette, and on the right a slightly larger alcove with room for a crib and a changing table. The place appeared empty to me, but Jackson crossed the room to the door by the alcove and pulled it open to reveal a tiny bathroom.

On the floor was a prone woman, with vomit coming out of her mouth.

"Fuck. Call an ambulance," Jackson ordered me, pulling on disposable gloves he'd conjured from his pocket as he rushed to help the woman. Since I didn't want to watch him put his fingers into her mouth to clear her airway, I took out my phone and called 911. "Is she breathing?" I asked him when the dispatcher on the other end asked it of me.

"Yes, but barely."

I relayed the information and then all we could do was wait. Jackson remained with Melody, constantly tapping her cheeks to keep her breathing, so I guessed a heroin overdose, as it messed with the part of brain that controlled breathing. Was it because her baby had been kidnapped? A twinge of sadness constricted my heart.

I made a quick study of the place. There was baby formula in the kitchen, but the cupboards and the fridge were almost empty. There were some clothes in two cardboard boxes by the sofa-bed, most of them the skimpy professional variety Melody used as a stripper. The alcove was more interesting. The crib was new and, even though I wasn't an expert, looked expensive. The bedclothes on it were clean and of good quality, and there were so many stuffed toys in it I wondered where the baby would fit. A mobile that played a lullaby hung above it. Next to it was a drawer full of baby clothes and other necessities; there was a diaper genie instead of a regular trash can, and the diapers on the changing table were brand names and not the cheaper store varieties, as were the lotions and powders. It didn't take a genius to figure out Melody prioritized her son in her spending.

The ambulance arrived and the paramedics did their best to stabilize Melody before whisking her away. There was nothing here for us, so we left too. We were closing the door, making sure it locked, when a woman spoke behind us:

"Who are you and what are you doing in my daughter's apartment?"

Chapter Eight

"MRS. BELL?" JACKSON ASKED, but the woman gave a derisive snort.

"Of course not. Melody Bell isn't my daughter's real name. I'm Kathy Morgan."

"And Melody's real name is...?"

"Joanna. Why she would choose that horrid name, I know not. Who are you?"

"I'm Jackson Dean. I'm a private detective and I'm afraid I have bad news for you. Your daughter was taken to the hospital with an overdose just now."

She staggered. "What about Robin?"

"Her son?" He sounded as surprised as I felt. Hadn't Melody—I couldn't think of her as Joanna—told her mother about the kidnapping? When the woman nodded, Jackson looked grave. "I think we'd best go inside to talk."

Mrs. Morgan had the key and she let us in. She glanced around, as if to verify our claim, and then sat heavily on the bed. "Just tell me."

"The reason we're here is that Robin has gone

missing," Jackson said carefully.

"Missing, how?"

"Kidnapped."

She paled at first, and then bright spots of fury rose to her cheeks. "I knew she wasn't fit to be a mother. I've told her time and again that she's useless, that she'll never manage with the baby, and I was right." Her tone was positively triumphant.

That wasn't exactly how I'd thought she'd take the news, but Jackson was better prepared. He picked a leaflet from the dining table I hadn't noticed when I went through the place. Some detective I was.

"I take it you brought this ad for a private adoption service here?"

The woman nodded, looking annoyingly self-righteous. "Yes. It's bad enough she's wasting her life as a ... a stripper," she spat the word out. "But with the baby she'll never amount to anything more."

Jackson frowned. "But you support her financially?"

She huffed. "Absolutely not. She got herself into this mess, she can sort it out."

"Then how can she afford all this?" I had to ask, waving at the baby-stuff. "They're pretty expensive."

"Must be that boyfriend of hers."

"Robin's father?" Jackson asked, though Steve had told the opposite.

"Hardly. I doubt she even knows the father. No, she's

sleeping with her drug dealer. I bet the bastard has money to spare."

"Even for a baby that isn't his?" Jackson asked, but the woman just shrugged. "Do you have a picture of Robin we could use?"

There were none in the apartment, which I found curious, as in my experience new mothers filled their homes with photos of their babies. But perhaps they were all in Melody's phone.

Mrs. Morgan frowned. "What for? If he's been kidnapped, he's already in the hands of some illegal adoption service instead of going through legit hands like he should have." But she went to fetch Melody's handbag. A short rummage of its contents produced Melody's phone, which she gave to Jackson.

"You can keep it for now. It's not like she needs it in the hospital." Then she slumped. "I guess I'd best head there myself. Which one was she taken to?"

Jackson gave her the name. "Where can we reach you if we need to ask more questions?"

"I work at the maternity clinic on Ocean Parkway. You can reach me there during the day."

I perked. "My mom works there too. Laura Hayes?"

She smiled, almost delighted. "Of course. You're the spitting image of her." I kind of was, too. Then she sighed. "I must be on my way now. Thank you for calling the ambulance."

A moment later she was out the door without waiting for us to follow. Since we didn't have a reason to stay, we exited the apartment too—again making sure the door locked—and headed back to Jackson's car.

"That was unpleasant," Jackson said once we were in the car.

I let my upset about Mrs. Morgan's behavior finally show. "An understatement. What sort of person would feel so little about her grandson disappearing? And she's a maternity nurse to boot." My mom would be furious and do anything to find her grandchild.

Jackson shook his head. "I know. But at least we have someone to look into."

"The boyfriend?"

"Yep." He opened Melody's phone and began to scroll the caller IDs. "One of these numbers has to belong to him."

It wasn't difficult to guess which one. There were at least twenty calls made to someone named Bruno since the previous day, all unanswered. "I take it this is him. I bet Melody's been calling him ever since the baby went missing."

"He hasn't answered. Do you think he took the baby?"

Jackson shook his head. "I see no reason why he would want to. But let's check him out anyway."

A quick search of the number gave us a name, Bruno

Schatz, but no address. "I'll call someone in Narcotics. If he's the drug dealer Mrs. Morgan mentioned, I'm sure they'll know him."

"Detective Lawrence?" I asked hopefully, and he grinned.

"Why not."

We'd met the detective during a case a while back and had helped him to bring down a drug smuggling operation. He owed us. Though that wasn't the reason I wanted Jackson to call him.

"Turns out we're in luck," Jackson said with a satisfied grin after the call ended. "They've had Schatz in custody since yesterday."

"No wonder he didn't answer Melody's calls." I sighed. "She probably wouldn't have OD'd if he had."

"We don't know that."

But I felt I was right. "So when he wouldn't answer, she went to Steve?"

"Most likely."

"But why didn't she go to her mom?"

Jackson gave me a slow look. "Did you not meet her just now? I bet Melody knew help wasn't forthcoming in that direction."

"Poor thing. Her only options were a drug dealer and a slouch."

"At least the slouch had the good sense to come to us," Jackson said, starting the car and pulling into traffic.

The 75th Precinct was in the easternmost neighborhood of Brooklyn called East New York, a place where good girls shouldn't wander alone. Drugs weren't necessarily the biggest problem there; poverty was, and hopelessness, which bred all sorts of ills, like organized crime. The station was a gem of Brutalist style and looked like a bunker, which I guess reflected the needs of the neighborhood.

Detective Tom Lawrence was a gem of a different variety entirely, a suave god made of chocolate, all six-foot-three of him. Today he'd covered his leanly muscled body with a dark suit and a slim-fit shirt that didn't force me to guess what was beneath it. Not that I wasn't perfectly able to imagine it. Which I instantly did when I laid eyes on him.

"Do I need to have your head scanned again?" Jackson asked, exasperated.

"I thought we agreed it was a sign of my brain functioning normally if I ogled the good detective," I countered, and then gave the man in question a sheepish grin.

"Sorry. Seems I can't help it."

His smug smile would've been annoying if it hadn't been so well deserved. "No problem. I take it your face is why you've had your head scanned?"

"Yeah." I gave him the brief version, which wiped the smile from his face.

"Is that why you want to talk to Bruno Schatz?"

"No, this is actually important." He cocked a nicely groomed brow, so I told him. "His girlfriend's baby has been kidnapped. We need to ask him if he knows anything about it."

"Fuck. Then you'd better talk with him right away."

He led us to an interview room and had someone bring Schatz over. He was in his mid to late twenties, tall, thin and weasely-looking, with shifty eyes that wouldn't look straight into anyone's—or maybe I was projecting. He hadn't shaved since the previous day and his clothes had seen better days.

Detective Lawrence allowed Jackson to handle the interview, a professional courtesy he hadn't given us the previous time we'd been here. "Do you know a woman named Joanna Morgan?" Jackson asked after introducing himself. That didn't get any reaction from Bruno. "Maybe you know her as Melody Bell?"

"Maybe."

"What about her son, Robin?"

This earned Jackson a puzzled look. "Have you arrested me because of the rugrat?"

"What do you think of him?"

"It's a baby, what's there to think? He's quiet most of the time and then cries at the most inopportune moment."

"Such as?"

"Sex." *Duh* was implied in his comment.

"When was the last time you saw Melody and her baby?"

He shrugged. "Last week, maybe. It's not like we're going steady."

"Then why has she called you twenty times since yesterday afternoon?"

"How should I know, I've been locked here, haven't I. What's this about?"

Jackson gave him an assessing look. "Robin has been kidnapped."

Bruno pulled back, pale. "Fuck. How's Melody taking it?"

"She's hospitalized with an overdose."

"I don't doubt it. She loves that boy. Only the best for him."

"Did you give her the money for his upkeep?"

"Why the fuck would I do that? He's not my kid."

"Then who did?"

"Some woman."

"Her mother?"

Bruno gave a derisive snort. "Hell no, the bitch wouldn't lift a finger to help her."

Jackson lifted his brows. "The two of them don't get along?"

"Her mother goes on and on about how she's seen too many women like Melody in her work ruin their lives because of a child. She's constantly pushing Melody for adoption, but she wouldn't do that. She's nuts about that boy."

"Do you have a name for the generous woman?"

"No. I've had no reason to ask."

I was pretty sure the guy had nothing to do with Robin being kidnapped, and so was Jackson, because he nodded and got up. I followed suit with Detective Lawrence.

"Not your guy?" the detective asked once we were out of the interview room. Jackson shook his head.

"But at least we know there's another player involved. The mystery woman who's paying for Robin's upkeep."

I gave him a puzzled look. "Why would she kidnap him?"

"Why would anyone kidnap a baby?" He sounded angry again, so I placed a placating hand on his arm and he pulled himself together. "Maybe she thinks he's her baby and just took him."

I nodded. "So we hope one of the numbers in Melody's phone belongs to her?"

"Sounds like a plan." He took out Melody's phone and searched the caller IDs. "Quite a few women here."

"But most of them have stripper names," I said, checking them over his shoulder.

"Then how about this? MC."

"Master of ceremony? Maybe it's her boss at the strip club."

"No, that's filed as 'boss'," Jackson noted. "Everyone else is clearly labeled, so why not this one?"

"Secrecy?"

"Exactly." He gave the phone to Detective Lawrence, who made a quick job of searching the number. We could've done it too, but it wasn't strictly speaking legal. No need to flaunt our methods in front of a cop.

"It belongs to Margaret Clark. Ring any bells?"

Jackson and I exchanged stunned looks. "You don't think...?"

He nodded. "Steve's mom."

Chapter Nine

"**W**HY WOULD SHE KIDNAP her own grand-child?" I asked, incredulous.

"Because she wanted him and her son wouldn't do anything to get custody?" Jackson suggested. Remembering the slouch, I could sort of believe it. "We have to go to her immediately."

"Hang on," Detective Lawrence interrupted. "If this woman's kidnapped the baby, it's a police matter."

Jackson nodded. "I agree, but first we need to find out if she actually has him."

"Surely she wouldn't just have him out in the open for anyone to notice?" I asked. Jackson and Detective Lawrence exchanged glances.

"She might, if she simply introduces him as her grandson," Jackson suggested, and the detective nodded too. I didn't believe them.

"But wouldn't Steve have noticed?"

"Does he still live at home?"

Since I didn't know the answer, we decided to go to meet Mrs. Clark without the police. But we promised that if we suspected she was hiding Robin somewhere, we would keep an eye on her and track her to the baby and then call the police.

Mrs. Clark lived in Prospect Heights, only a couple of blocks from our agency, which would explain why her son had chosen us to find his child. The classic nineteenth century brownstone townhouse looked elegant in the late afternoon sun, even with the trees almost bare of leaves and its age visible on its walls. The street sides were filled with expensive cars.

We took the high front steps to the door and rang the bell. The door was soon opened by a woman in her mid-forties, and well-preserved at that. Her makeup was flawless, as was her blond hair that was recently done in a short bob. She was wearing elegant black pants and a short-sleeved, light blue cashmere sweater, with large pearls around her neck and on her ears. Shoes were conservatively low. In short, she didn't in any way look like she'd been taking care of an infant.

My heart sank, but I wouldn't give up. The baby wasn't necessarily here, or she could've hired a nanny.

"Mrs. Clark?" Jackson asked in his polite voice and showed her his P.I. card. "May we have a word?"

"What's this about?" Her voice was elegant and a tad haughty.

"Your grandson."

She perked, delighted. "Are you from the lawyer? They did say there would be a surprise visit coming, but I didn't quite expect you on Thanksgiving weekend."

"No, I'm afraid I have bad news. Your grandson has been kidnapped."

All color left the woman's face and her knees gave under her. She would've dropped on the floor if Jackson hadn't acted swiftly. He took a good hold of her and helped her into the nearest chair in the elegant foyer.

"I'm sorry, I shouldn't have blurted it out like that," he said, sounding contrite, but I knew he had done it on purpose to get her reaction. I'd say she was genuinely shocked by the news. No one was that good an actor. She collected herself fairly fast though, and got up.

"I think it's best we talk in the living room. It's more comfortable there."

She led us to a lightly furnished room that gave on to the back yard, and went straight to a crystal decanter that stood on a side table. "Whisky?"

I wouldn't have minded a sip of what would most likely be the best stuff I'd ever taste, but Jackson shook his head. "Not on duty. But you have a glass. You'll need it."

She poured herself a hefty dose and then sank heavily on one of the cream-colored leather sofas facing each other. We sat opposite her. "Just tell me."

"I'm afraid we don't know the particulars yet. Melody—or Joanna, if you prefer—was hospitalized today and we haven't been able to ask her. But we understand that he was taken sometime yesterday."

"And why are you looking into it and not the police?"

"She didn't want to involve the police for the fear they'd declare her an unfit mother."

"*I'll* have her declared unfit for this."

"Is that why you've contacted lawyers?" Jackson inquired.

"Yes. I want my son to file for sole custody."

"And what does your son want?" I had to ask. I couldn't imagine that the slouch would want to become a full-time dad.

"That's irrelevant. He'll do as I tell him to."

Since her son hadn't bothered to tell her that the child had been kidnapped in the first place, she'd be in for a surprise. But I didn't want to disillusion her, so I kept my mouth shut.

"You have been paying for the child's upkeep," Jackson stated, as if we knew it for a fact, and Mrs. Clark nodded.

"Joanna can barely manage the rent. I had to do something. But I haven't given her any money, if that's what you're saying. I've bought everything for her. Otherwise, who knows what she'd use the money on?"

"And what do you get in return?"

"I get to see my grandson twice a week, Thursdays and Sundays."

"Yesterday was Thursday."

"Yes, but with the Thanksgiving, we rescheduled." Her face crumbled. "Maybe he wouldn't have been taken if we'd kept to our regular day."

"Where do you usually meet?"

"At a playground near her home."

"Albemarle?"

"I don't know its name. The one across the street from her home."

"At what time?" She raised a carefully plucked brow at my question, so I continued: "We don't have a timeline at the moment. Maybe she went there at your regular time."

"I don't think so. We usually meet around one in the afternoon, but I believe she said she would go to her mother's for the day when I invited her here."

Jackson and I both frowned. If Melody had gone to her mom's, her mother hadn't said anything about it. Perhaps the baby hadn't been taken from the playground, but later that day when Melody was returning from her mother's. We'd have to talk to Kathy Morgan again to ask for more details.

The front door was opened and closed loudly. "Mom, I'm home!"

Mrs. Clark wiped her cheeks quickly, just in time before Steve showed up in the living room door. He startled when he saw us.

"What are you doing here?" he asked. His mother didn't find the question odd, or that it would imply he knew us already.

"Oh, Steve, I have horrible news. Robin has been kidnapped."

The boy looked baffled, probably wondering why we hadn't told her he'd hired us in the first place. "Okay?"

"Okay? Is that all you have to say? Your son is gone!" She looked livid, but Steve just shrugged.

"Yeah, whatever. I'll be in my room. We have a great WoW raid starting." He disappeared from the door and a moment later his footsteps could be heard stomping up the stairs. A door banged open and shut again.

"I really don't understand what's wrong with that boy," his mother lamented. "It's most unnatural not to care about his own child. The only thing he has energy for is that hideous video game."

"He doesn't have any relationship with his son?" I asked.

"None whatsoever, and not because I haven't tried. I even invited Joanna and her son here once, but Steve wouldn't come out of his room. He's always there. He barely bothered to come down for dinner yesterday."

"He played the whole day?" I tried to sound incredulous rather than someone gouging for his whereabouts the previous day.

"Yes. All I could hear from him was what he talked to a microphone, and it wasn't suitable for Thanksgiving."

So he probably hadn't snuck out and kidnapped his child in order to get rid of him. It had been a long shot anyway.

Mrs. Clark picked up a framed photo from a side table next to her and stared at it through the tears that were clouding her eyes. "This was taken when Robin was visiting here." She handed the photo to me.

It was taken in the back garden. The day was sunny, the lawn was still green, and the quilt on it was colorful. A young woman was sitting on it, smiling hesitantly at the camera, holding an infant in pretty clothes on her lap. Melody, I presumed. She was prettier than I'd thought when I saw her earlier, but then again, she hadn't been at her best. The baby was kind of cute, like all babies were, and if there was resemblance to either of his parents I couldn't see it. I'd skimmed a couple of photos on Melody's phone on our way here, and this one looked like the baby in those photos, so I knew he was Robin.

Then I noticed the baby carriage in the background and blood fled to my ankles. If I hadn't been sitting down, I would've fallen.

"What is it?" Jackson immediately demanded, worried. Trust him to notice. "Is your head aching?"

"Yes," I said, seizing the opportunity. "I think we have to go."

Jackson took our leave and practically marched me out of the house. There I paused, gasping for breath, fighting nausea.

"Spill it," Jackson demanded.

"It was the baby carriage in the photo," I managed to say.

"What about it?"

"It was the same as the one from Trevor's crime scene yesterday."

He blanched. "Are you saying…?"

"Robin is the dead baby."

Chapter Ten

W E WENT STRAIGHT TO TREVOR. I thought to call him first, but the mere notion of relaying the news over the phone distressed me, so we drove to his precinct on Lawrence Avenue instead. It was already evening, but I wasn't surprised to see he was still there.

"I thought I told you to go home," I said when we reached his desk. He rubbed his face, tired.

"I can't face my son like this," he said. "What brings you here?"

"We may have the identity of your baby victim."

He perked. "Really? How?"

I gave him a quick recap of our research. "I only have the baby carriage to go by though. But does this baby look like him?" I showed him a picture of Robin from Melody's phone. He closed his eyes tightly and nodded. To be sure, he opened a casefile on his desk and compared my photo with a photo in there.

"Looks like him, but I'll need someone to make the official identification. The mother is hospitalized?"

"Yes," Jackson said, "and I'm not sure it would be wise to bother her with this until we're absolutely sure it's her child."

"Perhaps Mrs. Morgan could do it?" I suggested, and Trevor nodded.

"That'll have to do. Do you have anything else for me? A timeline? Where the baby was taken?"

"Nothing whatsoever yet, as we didn't have a chance to talk with Melody, and no one else seems to have a clue," Jackson said, aggravated.

"Any suspects?"

"We've basically ruled out the obvious ones. Her boyfriend was in custody and the child's father has an alibi. We briefly considered the paternal grandmother, but she'd recently begun legal procedures to have custody and I don't see why she would kidnap the baby."

"So this is just one more of those recent kidnappings gone wrong." Trevor's shoulders slumped. "The detectives investigating those don't have clues either."

"Maybe at this point they should all be investigated by a single team," I suggested.

"Yeah. If only we had resources for that."

"Jackson and I could do it."

"This is a murder investigation now."

"Yes, but it's *your* murder investigation. You could request the other cases and then outsource it to us."

He shook his head. "I doubt we have the money for it.

Besides, you've done what your client asked you to do—found the baby."

Not exactly how I'd wanted to find him. "We won't know for sure until we've had a positive ID."

"So let's get it done."

The morgue isn't exactly the kind of place you want to end your day in, especially if you're still alive. I'm fairly sure the dead didn't care, but if they did get a say, they'd probably say it sucked to end up there at any time of the day.

The body of the baby had been taken to the morgue of the nearest hospital to the crime scene, the Kings County Municipal Hospital. It formed the other half of the same hospital complex as the University Hospital of Brooklyn, where Tessa worked, the two separated only by Clarkson Avenue, but I'd never had any cause to visit there before.

It was also the same hospital where they'd taken Melody, so it saved us the trouble of hunting down her mother. We only had to locate Melody's room and she was there, sitting by her bed, holding her prone hand. Whatever she thought of her daughter's skills as a mother, she appeared to be a fairly dependable herself.

We weren't allowed into her room, but from Melody's doctor we learned that she'd been stabilized and that she was now sleeping. He strongly advised against waking her up in order to take her to identify the body.

"She was frantic about her baby when she woke up. We had to sedate her. If the body turns out to be her baby, it might push her over the edge."

We heartily agreed, as did Mrs. Morgan when we told her what we wanted. Her face was gray, but her step was steady as we crossed the huge hospital to the other end, where the morgue was. I'd never been to a morgue before, but based on TV I had a notion of clean, clinical spaces and cold storages. I was confident I could handle it, but when I pushed through the swinging double doors that separated it from the rest of the basement hallway, my heart started beating erratically and I had trouble breathing. By the time we reached the offices of the morgue personnel, my face had turned pale and I was sweating profusely. I dropped onto a chair outside the offices and refused to move.

Jackson and Trevor gave me worried looks, but I waved them on. Mrs. Morgan would need their support much more than I did. They followed the medical examiner, and a helpful morgue technician brought me a plastic cup filled with water.

"Don't feel bad. Many people find this place creepy."

"I thought I'd be able to handle it. It's not like I'm witnessing an autopsy or anything. And I've seen dead bodies before."

"It's not the death, it's the sorrow of those left behind that's getting to you."

He was likely right, because when Mrs. Morgan returned moments later, her face pale and leaning heavily against Jackson, my insides constricted so tightly my heart almost stopped. Jackson helped her to a chair and the technician brought her water too. She didn't drink it.

"How...?" It was all she managed to say, but the medical examiner who had followed them understood her just fine.

"Likely asphyxiation, but could be SIDS. Crib death," she clarified, her expression more sympathetic than her fictional counterparts' on TV.

"So if it wasn't SIDS, it was deliberate?" Trevor asked.

"There are no outward signs that he was suffocated, but it doesn't really take any force to suffocate a baby."

"My grandson was not murdered!" Mrs. Morgan shrieked. "It was an accident."

Trevor's eyes sharpened. "Do you know something about it?"

"I know nothing. But my daughter would never harm her son."

"So you're saying that the child died and then your daughter left him in the park?"

"Why would she do that?"

I could think of a reason: she didn't want her mother to know that she'd been right about her parenting skills all along. But I didn't think that's what happened. "Did your daughter spend the day with you yesterday?" I asked. She gave me a baffled look for the change of topic.

"Yes. It was Thanksgiving."

"When did she return home? We're trying to establish a timeline."

"It was early evening. I had a night shift at the hospital where I sub sometimes, so we dined early."

"And how did she go home? By bus?"

"No, she walked. I live only a couple of blocks from her place."

"How did she seem to you when she left? Happy, preoccupied?" In an urgent need for a fix that would cause her to not pay enough attention to her son's safety?

She frowned. "I didn't notice. Robin was being fussy, crying a lot. He's colicky, you know. So she was preoccupied, I guess, and tired. She doesn't get much sleep."

Perhaps she had stopped to sit on a bench some-where and fallen asleep. But Steve had said she'd been passed out. Had he misunderstood?

"I'm guessing her work doesn't help either?" Jackson asked.

"Definitely not. She's at work all night and then tries to sleep during the day, but Robin needs—" She paused and swallowed. "Needed ... attention."

"Who looked after him when she was at work?"

"Her next-door neighbor, Mrs. Paige. And sometimes she takes him—took him—to her work when Mrs. Paige wasn't available. But her boss didn't really like it when she did that."

Jackson and I exchanged glances. Mrs. Paige was definitely the person to talk to. Provided Trevor didn't try to keep us from investigating. My brother placed a hand on Mrs. Morgan's shoulder.

"Thank you, you've been very helpful. And I'm very sorry for your loss. Do you want me to break the news to your daughter?"

She shook her head. "No, I'll do it. Or ask her doctor to, just in case."

We walked her back to her daughter's ward and stayed while Dr. Frick broke the news to Melody. As predicted, she became hysterical, her screams audible through the closed door. I wanted to press my hands to my ears to escape, but I forced myself to listen. Soon enough they quieted, the doctor having sedated her again. When he exited the room, Trevor gave him his card.

"Please let me know when she's strong enough to answer some questions."

The doctor shook his head. "That won't be until sometime tomorrow, and even then only with medical supervision."

Trevor didn't look happy. "Is there any way we could ask a question now? Just to get the investigation going?"

"No, she's out cold and will remain so for the time being."

I wrapped my arm around Trevor's waist, even though he didn't appreciate familial gestures at work. "Come, let's talk with the neighbor. Then someone needs to break the news to Mrs. Clark."

"We need to establish the timeline," he said, not allowing me to move him.

"I know, and we will. Tomorrow."

He didn't like it—this was a murder investigation now and time was of the essence—but he knew better than to argue with a doctor. So we left the hospital and drove to Melody's building. It was getting late, but if Mrs. Paige was willing to babysit during nights, she was probably still awake.

But when Trevor knocked on the door it was opened by a man in his late twenties. He took one look at us and threw the door closed on our faces. Before we could so much as blink, we heard a window being opened in the apartment.

Trevor didn't hesitate. He drew his weapon, kicked the door open, and charged after the guy. Jackson ran down the way we'd come, presumably to intercept the guy on the street where the fire escape led. I was left standing in the hallway with my mouth agape.

Chapter Eleven

I FELT NO COMPUNCTION ENTERING the apartment. The door was open, after all. The fire escape creaked and clanged with the weight of two men descending it, but I had no doubt Trevor would catch the guy. So instead of hurrying to the window to watch, I made a quick study of the apartment.

The main room was much like Melody's, except that it was a mirror of it, and stuffed full of furniture that had clearly been bought for a much larger place. A small army could be hiding behind the sofas and armchairs and I wouldn't even see them. Then again, they wouldn't be able to move fast enough to attack me with all the end tables and floor lamps blocking the way. The alcove had a narrow single bed with a handmade quilt covering it, and the kitchenette was clean, apart from a couple of pizza boxes and a twelve-pack of empty beer cans on the counter. The bathroom was empty.

Unlike in Melody's apartment, this one had a bedroom behind the kitchenette. A wide double bed took up most of the space. What was left was piled ceiling-high with cardboard boxes, all unopened, with pictures of cell phones, laptops, and other portable consumer electronics on them. Explained why the guy had run.

I returned to the main room, where I found a note on the dining table from "Mom"—presumably Mrs. Paige—about the food in the fridge the guy was meant to subsist on until she returned on Sunday. I checked the fridge, but the food there hadn't been touched. Either she was a lousy cook or her son was too lazy to warm it up. Judging by the number of pizza boxes on the counter, she'd been away since the day before yesterday. My shoulders slumped: there went the hope that Mrs. Paige would know something.

Trevor and Jackson returned, dragging Mrs. Paige's cuffed son between them. "He refuses to talk," Trevor said with a sneer. He was barely out of breath.

"He doesn't have to. Look in the bedroom." They took a peek and let out appreciative whistles.

"They're not mine," the guy stated defiantly.

"I know. So what are they doing here?" Trevor asked.

"I'm holding them for a friend."

"While your mother is away?" I pitched in.

Trevor stifled a curse. "How long has she been gone?"

The guy looked puzzled. "Since Wednesday. She went to grandma's for the holidays."

"Didn't you want to join her?" I asked, but the guy

just rolled his eyes. "What do you know about the woman next door?"

"Melody?" When I nodded, an appreciative smile spread on his face. "She's hot. I'd try her if it weren't for the kid. He's got some pipes on him. Never stops crying. Colicky says my mom. She looks after him."

"Was she home yesterday?"

"Was she ever. I was trying to sleep, but the kid just wouldn't stop crying. She was carrying him around the whole day, singing lullabies and whatnot. The place only quieted, like, at two in the afternoon."

I frowned. "That's when they left?"

"No, the baby fell asleep. Anyways, I didn't hear her taking that fancy baby carriage down the stairs. There's no elevator, so she bumps it down from step to step. Makes a lot of noise."

"So she stayed at home the whole day?"

He made to rub his face, noticed the cuffs and thought better of it. "Yeah. She had a visitor around two-thirty though. That's when I got up."

"How do you know?"

"I heard them insert the key. Probably best that they didn't knock, because the kid was finally sleeping." Then he frowned. "But the visitor left with the baby carriage five minutes later. That I definitely heard." He mimicked pushing the carriage down the stairs one step at a time.

"How do you know it wasn't Melody?"

"Because she started screaming maybe an hour later. I hadn't heard anyone return, so she couldn't have left."

That was astute of him.

"What was she screaming about?" Jackson asked.

"How should I know? I mind my own business."

Such chivalry.

Uniformed cops arrived to take the guy away and process the stolen goods, ending our interview. We'd likely gotten what we could from him anyway, so we left. Trevor went straight to Melody's door, took out a flashlight and pointed it at the lock.

"It's not been picked or damaged, so the visitor did have a key."

"Melody's mother had one," I said. Jackson and Trevor stared at me, stunned.

"Why would she take her grandson?" Jackson asked, incredulous.

"I'm not saying she did. But either she's lying or that fence-in-making is. She said Melody was at her place until early evening, but the guy says she stayed home. And we already know that the body was found in the afternoon, so Robin couldn't have been alive when Mrs. Morgan said."

Trevor nodded. "He was found around half past three. And he hadn't been dead all that long."

Jackson summed up: "So someone ghosts away with the kid around twenty to three and forty-five minutes later, maybe less, he's dead?"

I felt sick. "Who would know about the child to take him from his home?"

"Apart from Melody's mother?" Jackson asked, and I nodded. "Steve's mother."

"But we already ruled her out."

"We only have her word that she spent the day at home. Steve can't provide an alibi, having spent the day gaming in his room. And we mainly ruled her out because she had other means of getting her hands on him."

We headed down the stairs and to Trevor's car, deep in thought. "Maybe Mrs. Clark didn't intend to take him," Trevor suggested. "Maybe she was feeling lonely and decided to visit Robin and Melody. She finds the two of them sleeping and—I don't know—maybe decides to give Melody a break by taking Robin out for a stroll. Only something goes wrong and the child dies. She panics and abandons the carriage in the park."

It made a horrible kind of sense. "That doesn't explain why Mrs. Morgan would lie about Melody being with her."

Trevor cranked the engine. "Let's tackle one question at a time. I need to speak with Mrs. Clark."

It was almost ten in the evening by the time we reached her townhouse, but the lights were on so we didn't hesitate ringing the doorbell. The lady of the house opened the door. She took one look at us and paled. "You have bad news."

Trevor took charge. "Yes. I'm Detective Hayes from the NYPD. May we come in?"

"Yes, of course." She led us to the living room, where Steve was watching TV. "Shut that thing off," she ordered, and the boy complied. "Please, take a seat."

We did. Trevor spoke. "I'm sorry to tell you, but your grandson is dead."

Tears sprang to Mrs. Clark's eyes and even Steve staggered. "How?" she asked.

"The exact cause of death is unknown, but SIDS isn't ruled out."

"Why would you say he was kidnapped, then?"

"Because that's what the mother said. And the body was found abandoned in the park."

She stared at us unbelieving for a few heartbeats. Then she turned to Steve, furious. "This would never have happened if you'd just done your duty and filed for custody like I told you."

He looked baffled. "If he died of natural causes, how could I have prevented it?"

"At least he wouldn't have been abandoned in the park." She started crying. If she was responsible for his death, she was a really good actor. Her grief was painful to look at.

I cleared my throat. "Steve, could I have a word with you in private?" I got up and went into the hall. He followed me. "I'm sorry for your loss," I started, and had the satisfaction of seeing some grief in his eyes.

"Yeah. I didn't really care for the kid, but Mother did."

"I understand you spent the entire day yesterday on your computer?"

He blushed. "Not very dutiful of me, huh?"

"*World of Warcraft?*"

"Yeah."

I nodded. "My roommate plays it too. What character do you play?"

"A human mage for the Alliance called Arugal."

I made a mental note of the name. "And your mother spent the day all alone?"

"Well, there was Consuela," he said defensively.

"And she would be?"

"The housekeeper. Mom likes to pretend she's a household goddess, but she merely sits in the kitchen and watches Consuela cook."

"Was she here the whole day?"

"Pretty much. We sat at the table around six, and she'd been cooking until then."

"Could I talk with her?"

"Sure." He led me to the end of the hallway and through a door on the left that opened onto a spacious, fully modernized kitchen. A Latina woman in her fifties was stirring something on the stove. "Good, you're still here," Steve said. "This is Tracy and she has some questions for you."

"Okay, but I have to keep stirring."

I waved her to continue. "I only have a couple of questions. Were you here the whole day yesterday?"

"Yes, I arrived at seven in the morning and left after eight in the evening."

"Long day," I noted, though it wasn't unusual. I'd worked similar days as a waitress.

"There was a lot of cooking to be done."

"For only two people?"

She shrugged. "Who am I to judge?"

"And what about Mrs. Clark? Was she home the whole day?"

"Yes she was. She wouldn't leave the kitchen. She was lonely." She shot an acerbic glance at Steve, who didn't even notice.

"So there were no afternoon walks or something?"

"No. She stuck here like glue."

I thanked her and returned to the hallway, where Trevor and Jackson appeared just then too. We left without arresting anyone.

"What did you learn?" Trevor asked.

"Mrs. Clark has an alibi. The housekeeper, Consuela, vouches for her."

"Shit."

I had nothing to add to that.

Chapter Twelve

WE FETCHED MISTY FROM THE OFFICE, where she'd slept most of the day and then gotten bored, upended the trash can and spread the contents all over the floor. She was sitting in the middle of the mess, looking proud of herself. We didn't have the energy to clean it up, so we just took her and headed back out. Trevor drove us to his precinct, where we'd left Jackson's car.

"Are you going home?" I asked my brother, who nodded.

"Might as well. It's not like we can do anything tonight."

I turned to Jackson. "Want to come too? There's bound to be plenty of turkey left."

"I don't want to impose on your mother," he hedged. Trevor and I snorted, making him smile. "Okay, but only because Mason really liked Misty."

Mom was happy to see us, but she said she'd expected us hours ago when they'd dined. Mason should've been in bed already, but he was ecstatic to see

Misty and wouldn't hear of it. Dad took one look at us, went to his secret stash, the location of which was passed from older sibling to younger one when we were deemed old enough to sneak in for a pre-party drink behind our parents' backs, and returned with a bottle of Irish whiskey. He was at least as patriotic as Thomas Thayne Westley drink-wise, but when it came to whiskey he was Irish through and through, as if his ancestors hadn't moved here a century ago already.

"For medicine." We didn't refuse.

Trevor went to put Mason to bed while I helped Mom set the table and Jackson sat with Dad in the living room. I heard them talking about the case. I was sure Mom didn't really want to hear about it, but I had questions for her.

"Do you know Mrs. Morgan? Works at your clinic."

"Yes, why?"

"It was her grandson whose death we've been investigating the whole day."

Tears sprang to her eyes and she sank heavily into a kitchen chair. "That's horrible. How's she taking it?"

"Not the way I thought she would be, which is why I wanted to talk with you."

"Is there more than one way to react to a death of a child?"

I'd seen two kinds of reactions today I hadn't exactly expected, and I didn't know which one I found worse.

"She seemed ... vindicated, as if the baby's death had confirmed all her expectations about her daughter as a mother." Mom stiffened and I instantly latched onto it. "You're not surprised."

She sighed. "She's been reprimanded more than once about how she treats the poorer mothers. She thinks they're unfit for keeping their children, that poverty is heritable and it's immoral to pass it on to the next generation. She's a strong advocate of adoption and doesn't hide it from those mothers. Some have left quite distressed from their appointments with her."

"She tried to do that to her daughter too."

"She would never!" Mom was outraged. "That's ... I mean ... her own grandchild!"

I patted her hand. "None of your grandchildren will ever be given away, including the devil spawns."

That got a small smile from her. "They're not that bad. You'll understand when you have your own kids."

"That's not likely to happen anytime soon." If ever, but I thought it best not to say that aloud.

"Maybe you should do like Mason's mother and get pregnant by some handsome fellow you'll never see again."

"Mom!" I was scandalized. That was not what I would've thought she'd ever say.

"You're clearly not interested in seeing anyone, so why not? How about Jackson?"

My mouth fell open. "No!"

"Why not? He's handsome."

"Yes, but he wouldn't be out of my life, and I need him in it more than I need a child." This conversation was getting uncomfortable, but Mom's smile was happier.

"Keep it in mind."

"I so will not." I ended the conversation by marching to the living room and sitting next to Jackson on the sofa. He wrapped an arm around my shoulders.

"How are you holding up?"

I leaned against him. "Well enough. But I can't decide if I want to see this through or never think about it again."

Trevor spoke from the door. "I hope you haven't changed your mind about participating, because my boss just called. Since it's probable that Robin's death is linked to the kidnappings, they've given all those cases to me. I'll need your help."

I was instantly energized. "I'm in."

Jackson squeezed my shoulder. "We'll find who's behind this."

I really hoped he was right.

"You were supposed to have the weekend off," Dad said to Trevor, worried and disappointed. "For Mason."

Trevor rubbed his face, aggravated. "I know, Dad, but you know how it is with murder investigations."

"I have an idea," I intervened before the conversation

got out of hands. The two of them were capable of really good fights. "Why don't you spend the day at all the playgrounds where children have been taken. Listen to the mothers, ask questions if needed. Spend quality time with your son."

"That's a great idea," Trevor said, but Dad was less delighted.

"What if they take Mason?"

That was a real concern. "So far they've only taken babies from poor single mothers. Mason is older, and Trevor can let people understand that he's in a relationship with the mother and both are perfectly capable of providing for the kid, just in case the kidnapper is among the mothers."

"And I won't let him out of my sight for a moment," Trevor assured Dad.

Jackson gave me a lift home after the late dinner. Mom would've wanted me to stay the night, but I was out of clean underwear and other necessities. I lived in Midwood, less than two miles from my parents' house, but thanks to the transportation planning in this borough, there was no public transportation between the two locations. I occasionally borrowed my mom's cherry-red Ford Fiesta, but I was still under orders not to drive. Besides, my place was on Jackson's way home.

He pulled over outside the seven-story building where I lived at the corner of Ocean and J and cut the engine.

He usually waited just long enough to see that I got in safely before driving away, so I figured he had something to say.

"Are you sure you'll be okay alone?"

I gave it a thought. His concern was genuine and didn't deserve a flippant answer. "Yes, especially now that I know I'll be allowed to do something to catch whoever's behind this. You?"

He startled a bit, as if his emotional and mental state didn't require inquiring after. "Sure. Why wouldn't I be?"

"You've gotten really angry a couple of times today and that's not like you. This is personal to you in a way that I don't understand."

"Yeah," he admitted, but looked like he wouldn't continue, so I prompted him. He still took his time to answer, clearly organizing his thoughts to find the best answer. "Back when I started helping my uncle at the agency, before I joined the Marines, we had a similar case of a missing child where the parents didn't want to involve police. It was before the internet made everything easier, and we didn't have similar resources. We couldn't solve the case and the child was later found dead." His face distorted. "Sexual predator."

I felt sick. "Did you catch him?"

"The police did, no thanks to us."

"So you got angry because Melody didn't head straight to the best possible help?"

"I guess. I didn't exactly analyze the emotion."

I squeezed his shoulder. "It wouldn't have made any difference. The child was already dead and the police were already involved by the time you got the case. You just didn't know it. And now we have a chance to solve this."

He smiled. "And we will."

I smiled back. "So I'll ask again, are you okay being alone today."

"Yes. And I'm not alone. I have Misty."

I kind of envied him for her. "And I guess you can always call Emily if the solitude feels pressing."

"I don't think so."

My insides tensed. "Oh?"

He rubbed his face. "We're not that close. In fact, I'm going to end it."

"That's…" Great. "…sad," I opted with. I shouldn't have felt delighted, especially after I'd pushed them together myself, so I thought it best not to analyze my emotions either.

"Not really. I should've ended it ages ago, but something's always come up."

"Or you've chickened out."

He grinned. "Or that." He started the engine again and I took it as a cue to leave. "I'll pick you up at nine tomorrow."

"For work?"

"Do you want to postpone this over the weekend?"

"No, I just wanted to make sure you're not fetching me for a run, is all."

He laughed and I exited the car. He waited until I was inside before driving away. It felt nice to be looked after, even if this wasn't a bad neighborhood. The building was nice too, with its own janitor who kept the place clean and operational, and neighbors who didn't bother you overly much, if you didn't count the smells of exotic and not-so-exotic foods that often filled the hallways. It was also too expensive for me, but with a roommate I could manage the rent.

My apartment was on the fifth floor and I took the elevator, as the energy that had kept me going the entire day had finally deserted me. I barely had the strength to insert the key and open the door to my empty apartment.

Only it wasn't empty.

Chapter Thirteen

A SURGE OF ADRENALINE SHARPENED my senses and I paused on the threshold, letting the light from the hallway illuminate the dark apartment as I listened to what had alerted me to the presence of someone inside. A few frantic heartbeats brought clarity. I hit the lights, marched to my roommate's door, and threw it open.

"Jarod! What the hell are you doing here?"

He didn't react. He was sitting at his desk, his back turned to me, headphones over his ears. The room was dark save for the light that came from his computer screens, so I switched on the lights in there too. He shrieked in fright and almost fell off his chair in his attempt to face the door.

"Tracy, you almost gave me a heart attack," he managed to say, taking off his headphones. "What are you doing here?"

"What am I doing here? Weren't you supposed to be in Aruba with your parents over the holidays?"

Jarod was twenty-one, a grad student in computer

science at Brooklyn College a block away from our building, and a security expert at Lexton Security in Dumbo. Technically, he was a grownup who was allowed to do what he wanted, but that wasn't the point here. He'd told me clearly he would spend the weekend with his parents.

He ran fingers self-consciously through his overgrown mop of hair. He was tall and scrawny and tended to ignite what maternal feelings I had with his total inability to comprehend anything that wasn't computer related, but I wouldn't let him off easy this time. Even if he gave me a pleading look with his brown puppy dog eyes.

"I told them I had to work through the weekend."

"When instead you've stayed here, in the dark, playing the whole time?"

"We have a raid going," he defended himself.

"Then why couldn't you just tell me you were staying home?"

"Because you would've worried about me and insisted I join your family for dinner."

Since that was true, I had no comment. "Do you know Steve Clark?" I asked instead.

"Yes. He's one of our undergrads. I teach him occasionally. And he's part of our WoW raid."

I hadn't expected it to be that easy. "What character does he play?" I asked to make sure. Anyone could impersonate someone else online.

"This mage called Arugal. He's great."

"And I take it he's been playing the entire two days too without interruptions?"

"Pretty much."

That wasn't good enough. "Pretty much?"

"He had to have dinner with his mother at some point yesterday, and he popped off a couple of times today, but otherwise yes."

That confirmed Steve's alibi, then. "Mom gave me some leftovers. Come on, I'll heat them up for you."

THE NEXT MORNING, Jackson drove us straight to the hospital where Melody was being treated. "The doctor has cleared us to ask her some questions, but nothing distressing."

"Difficult to avoid that," I said, my heart aching in sympathy.

We found Melody alone, her mother not having arrived yet. She was calm, but her dilated pupils indicated it was medically induced. When we offered our condolences, she got tears in her eyes, but no stronger reaction than that. It was good from our point of view, but I felt horrified for her that she'd been robbed of her right to grieve the way she wanted.

It was just the two of us asking the questions, as Trevor trusted us to handle the interview without him. If it weren't for Mason occupying his time, I'd say he'd lost his mind. I was sitting in a visitor's chair next to Melody's bed, holding her hand that wasn't connected to IV tubes, and Jackson was standing at the side of the room, mostly out of her line of vision.

"Tell me about your Thanksgiving." We'd only been given a short time for this, so I went straight to the point.

"There's nothing much to tell. Robin woke up fussy around eight and nothing I did stopped him from crying. He's colicky. But he tired eventually and fell asleep propped up against my shoulder as I sat on my bed. I fell asleep, and when I woke up he wasn't there." Sheer animal panic flashed in her eyes for the memory, but the meds in her blood instantly subdued it.

"Had you made plans for the holidays?"

She gave me a tired look. "No. My mom and I don't really see eye to eye about Robin, and I didn't want to spend the day arguing with her."

"Then why would she tell us you'd spent the day with her?"

"Probably because it's what people expect. It's Thanksgiving. You're supposed to spend it with your family, no matter how much you hate each other. She was probably ashamed to admit the truth."

"Your mother hates you?" That wasn't the impression I'd gotten. She'd spent the day by her daughter's bedside after all. Unless that was only because that was expected of her too.

She shrugged. "I don't know if she hates me, but she

disapproves of me strongly, and in her world that's the same thing. I didn't manage to finish school and have to work as a stripper. But the worst insult to her worldview was when I became pregnant. She's done nothing but criticize my skills as a mother ever since Robin was born. I guess she was right."

She began crying silently.

I squeezed her hand. "What happened to Robin wasn't your fault. He was taken from the safety of your home. You didn't abandon him or mistreat him."

"But I fell asleep."

"You're allowed to sleep in your own home."

"I didn't wake up when some stranger walked into my home and just took him."

"You were exhausted. And I this person is really good at what they do. Other babies have gone missing too."

"From their homes?"

I actually didn't know the answer to that. "Mostly from parks," I admitted.

"So how come my baby was taken from my home?" She was getting more frantic now, the meds not working fast enough to counter it.

"That's what we'll find out," I said as convincingly as I could.

"Can you please at least tell me how my baby died? The doctors wouldn't tell me."

"That's because they don't know yet, but most likely

it was natural causes. No one deliberately harmed your child."

Apparently that was the right thing to say, because she closed her eyes and fell asleep between one heartbeat and the next. We left her to sleep.

At the office, we had to clear up the mess Misty had made, while she stood on the couch, watching us with a bemused look in her button eyes, occasionally barking at the broom. We'd barely finished when two uniformed cops from Trevor's precinct showed up with two boxes of case files and evidence for us. Either there were more children missing than I thought or I owed someone an apology for thinking they wouldn't investigate the cases thoroughly.

I hoped the latter was true. I wouldn't mind some mental groveling if it meant fewer children were taken.

The cops were followed in by Detective Kelley. "Officially this is Trevor's case now, but under my supervision. So you'd better keep me posted."

"Any insights to offer?" Jackson asked.

"I've talked with a friend of mine from the FBI who deals with child-trafficking. He promised to check the illegal adoption rings his people are investigating." We thanked her and she left, leaving us with the boxes.

"I guess there's nothing to it but to read these files through," Jackson said.

"What should I look for?"

"Any similarities between the cases. Anything that would connect the mothers or the children to each other. A dentist, a drug dealer, a nursery. Anything. Someone has to know all these children or their mothers somehow. They've been taken too close together from each other for them to have been chosen at random."

We each took a box and read every single file in it for similarities. We had a large map where we pinned the locations of the kidnappings and where the mothers lived. We made lists of everything, their professions— the few who worked—their ethnic backgrounds, where they shopped, even where they washed their clothes. I had to give it to the officers who'd worked the cases: they'd been thorough. The women were from a small area, so there was some overlapping, but nothing that would've matched to them all. The only thing they had in common was that they were all young, this was their first child, and they were raising the child alone.

"How many of them have criminal records?" Jackson asked when we were going through the data we'd sorted.

"A couple of them, petty thefts and drugs mostly."

"Maybe they used the same legal counsel."

"You're not seriously suggesting that a lawyer would be behind this?"

"At this point, I'm not ruling out anyone. But maybe the same lawyer consults a shadier adoption office too, and gives them information about clients with suitable babies."

We checked our tables, but not many of the mothers had needed to use a lawyer. "That we know of," Jackson said. "Perhaps we should talk with the women and ask."

"Absolutely. But first we should make a list of potential things that they could have in common but haven't been asked by the police."

We stared at the map and all the places the women could've shared: bus stops, drug stores and parks, fast food places, liquor stores, and unemployment offices. We consulted the borough administration and checked the services they might use, but they were from three different administrative areas despite living within a couple of square miles of each other.

"There's the school…" I pointed at the elementary that was within reach of all the women.

"The children were all babies."

"Perhaps the school has family activities."

"I'd suggest the church for that."

"They aren't all Christians."

"The Y?"

"Maybe." I made a note of it. "Blood bank?"

"Definitely worth checking. Free clinics?"

But when we checked them, it turned out that the only one that might have served all the women was the one my mother worked in.

Chapter Fourteen

"THAT'S UNFORTUNATE." And that was putting it mildly. It wasn't just the idea that a person connected to a place of healing might be behind it, it was thinking that someone close to my mother might be evil.

"We know it's not your mother behind this," Jackson said with a small smile. "There's enough love in her heart to spare for less fortunate kids too." He'd been one of them, but definitely not the only one.

"I know, but she'll be upset if it turns out to be the only thing the women have in common."

"Let's ask Melody first. She's the likeliest customer, because of her mother." He called the doctor treating Melody, who relayed the question to her.

"Ms. Morgan said she visited our hospital for her pre and postnatal care," Dr. Frick informed us a moment later. "Apparently her employer had insurance."

I staggered at the idea of a striptease joint having a pregnancy packet for their employees, but I was relieved too. My mother's clinic wasn't involved.

We made a list of the women's addresses and our questions, and were about to leave to take Misty for a walk and have a quick lunch when Detectives Newman and Migliaccio showed up.

"Good, you two have perverse schedules too, working on a Saturday," Pete greeted us affably. Then he noticed the maps and papers covering our notice board and whistled. "Big case?"

Jackson grimaced. "We're helping Trevor crack a series of abducted babies."

"Fuck. Then you probably won't have time to help us?"

"What would you need?"

"We've interviewed everyone present at Wednesday's party and no one, including the host, has seen this man." He waved the picture the sketch artist had made.

My heart fell. "Not even the caterer?"

"No, but we think the kitchen was the likeliest route in."

"Has it been the same caterer every time?"

"Not once."

I tried to remember the pre-party briefing the caterer had given us. Most of us had been temps, hired for that night only—well, I hadn't actually been hired, nor paid for my extra efforts, but only the caterer had known that.

"I don't remember him in the kitchen, but then again,

I don't remember seeing him among the guests either."

"What if he only walked in after the fire alarm went off?" Jackson suggested. "The kitchen staff evacuates, leaving the door open, and he comes in."

"If that's the case, he managed to steal a lot of stuff in a brief time," Detective Migliaccio mused. "But he can't have been long at it anyway, or the guests would've started to notice their missing valuables earlier."

"Maybe he simply waited for the party to be in full swing before he came in through the kitchen?" I said.

"That's possible too, but the fact remains that you're the only one who had a good look at the guy," Pete said. "Database search didn't yield anything, and the data people are still scouring the internet with the hopes that he turns out to be some minor league baseball player after all. But that's a long shot." We all nodded. "Anyway, that's why we came to you. There's a high profile party tonight that fits the thief's profile, and we want you there."

I blinked. "Me? As a waitress?" I'd rather chew my arm off.

"No, as a guest."

I blinked again. Then I glanced at Jackson and we both burst out laughing. "Right, 'cause I'd fit right in," I said when I managed to speak again, wiping my eyes. Jackson got serious too.

"How does this party fit the profile? I thought most of them were safe breaks."

Pete nodded. "We thought so too, but after this party we pooled the cases and it turned out there'd been a couple of similar robberies like this one before. Either they're linked or we have two brazen thieves out there. Either way, the party fits the bill for both."

"And you want me there?" Hysteria threatened to set in again. "How? And how the hell am I supposed to blend in?" I pointed at my face that had assumed some interesting colors today as the bruise began to fade. "I doubt any of the rich and shameless will show up with a black eye." And that was the least of my problems.

"Mr. Westley has been invited, and he's agreed to take you as his date. As for your face, we sometimes use the services of a makeup artist for undercover work. He'll take care of it. And your hair too," Pete added with a meaningful look at my cotton-candy-pink hair. "That's too memorable. Even if the thief doesn't remember your face, he'll remember your hair, so you'll wear a wig."

"That leaves my dress."

"I'm sure you have something in your closet," he said with a dismissing wave of his hand, as if LBDs suitable for an uptown party grew on trees. I definitely didn't own one, and I doubted I'd be able to squeeze into the only remotely suitable dress I had. It had been bought before my last waitressing job at the café, where free donuts had been the only perk. Besides, the last time I'd worn it I'd gotten into a fight and it hadn't escaped unscathed.

"I'll think of something." Namely Melissa. Her closets were full of suitable clothes, and with a stretch of imagination—or fabric—I might even manage to pull one of them on.

"Great. The makeup artist will come here at six, and Mr. Westley will fetch you at seven thirty."

"Hang on," Jackson interrupted. "What about her safety? We can't just assume that the thief won't recognize her. And where will I be?"

"You can't be at the party for the same reason she can't be recognized there. But we'll have her wired and you can hang out with us and listen in."

I could tell by Jackson's frown that he wasn't happy, but he nodded and the detectives left. "You don't have to do this if you don't want to," he said to me.

"Are you kidding me? A chance to see this kind of party from the other side? I wouldn't miss it for the world."

"Fine, but we'll go through some security measures first."

"Absolutely. But now, let's go interview the women."

There were seven women if you didn't count Melody—which was eight children too many kidnapped, if you asked me—from the area of three adjoining police precincts. The tenements they lived in had probably never seen good days, and a couple of them weren't really fit for living, let alone raising a kid. Melody had actually lived like a king compared to most of them. Most of the women didn't look much better than their abodes, but that didn't mean that each and every mother wouldn't have been devastated over losing their child.

"About damn time the cops are doing something," they all said, angry and tearful, when we introduced ourselves.

"Absolutely," Jackson said every time. "Unfortunately we didn't realize how many babies had gone missing until the cases were combined. If you could answer a few questions? We're trying to find what you all have in common."

"Apart from being piss poor and wasted out of our minds?" asked one who was currently fairly sober.

"Well, we would like to know who your drug dealer is," he said with a small smile. "We won't tell the cops, if it makes it easier to answer that one. Besides, one dealer is currently behind bars anyway." But only one woman turned out to have the same dealer as Melody; the others all listed different names.

"Small territories," I noted to Jackson at some point. "You'd think the opposite would happen after we took Brody out of the equation."

"Someone always steps in to fill the void."

I had a pretty good idea who it was. Craig Douglas,

the mobster we'd crossed paths with during the first case I worked on for Jackson. Not that we had any real evidence that he was a drug-dealing scumbag.

The women had some things in common, but never all of them. Four of them used the same thrift store, a different four the same launderette. Three had used the same lawyer and three others had taken their children to the same playground, but the rest had gone to different ones, and one of the women had never taken her child to a playground at all.

But as the day turned towards late afternoon, it was becoming increasingly obvious that, apart from Melody, they all had one thing in common: they'd used the services of the maternity clinic where my mother worked.

"I'd say that's our best bet," Jackson said when we were driving to my parents' around four after we'd talked to the last woman.

"But Melody didn't use it."

"Her mother works there, so that's a connection."

I didn't like it one bit, but I nodded. "How do you want to proceed?"

"We'll talk with Trevor. This is his case after all. Besides, we won't get our hands into any official records about the clinic without him."

"Okay, but not a word to Mom. She'd get upset."

"I couldn't tell her about a possible investigation

117

involving her workplace anyway."

"You think it's someone working there?" I felt like throwing up for the mere thought.

"I'd say it's much more likely than some random patient who's happened to be present at the same time with all those women. But it doesn't have to be any of the medical staff. It could be a janitor or a secretary just as well."

I'd keep my fingers crossed.

Chapter Fifteen

MY PARENTS' HOUSE WAS IN CHAOS that made me want to back out the moment I stepped in. Travis and Melissa had come over and brought the devil spawns for a visit. The twins had pulled Mason into play-time that involved running around the downstairs from the living room to dining room to kitchen to hallway and into the living room again, yelling as loudly as they could. Add Misty to that and it was a wonder no one got hurt.

While my parents supervised the kids, my brothers and sister-in-law had sought refuge in the living room. Travis rose to give me a warm hug, as we hadn't seen each other for a couple of weeks. The agency occasionally helped the Brooklyn Public Defender Service where he worked, but there had been no cases for us this month.

He was the spitting image of our father, six feet of lean muscle, dark Irish coloring, handsome, and dependable looking, which all served him well in his work as an assistant DA, as well as with his political aspirations. He had the young Kennedy vibe going, as I'd heard someone mention. I couldn't see it, but then again, he'd always been just my brother.

"Why did you have to bring the dog in?" he said with a frown after greeting me. Being eight years older than me, I'd always found him overly serious and pompous, but he was a good brother. "It'll only make the twins want one and I'm allergic to them."

"Which is a good reason why they can't have one," I said resolutely, as if I were an expert on child rearing. But really, it didn't take a genius to figure out the rule: "About time they learned they can't have everything they want."

I could see by the small crease that appeared between my sister-in-law's well-groomed brows that she didn't share my view, but she didn't say anything as she blew airy kisses near my cheeks—a trick I'd only learned when Travis had first started dating her eight years ago.

She was thirty-three and from a different world from us, with inherited money and all the trappings that came with it, like a beauty pageant past and an ivy-league education. She was tall and slim, with long blond hair she hadn't cut even when the twins were babies and constantly clinging to it. Her face was coolly beautiful and wrinkle-free. The green of her eyes was from contacts, but natural looking, and I knew she was considering a boob job to repair the damage the twins had caused to the girls, but only a tasteful lift.

She could've afforded to stay at home; she had private means to resort to even though Travis didn't make the kind of money he would've had as a partner in a law firm, but she worked at an upmarket art gallery in Manhattan. As far as I knew, she loved it. And since her father was the DA for Queens County and politically well-connected, she was the perfect wife for an aspiring politician.

Not that I doubted my brother hadn't married her for love. He'd been nuts about her when they first started dating. These days, I didn't know. They were both re-served, and the twins were a handful. I knew he worked late most days, which couldn't be good for their marriage.

"Thank you for helping me out," I said when Melissa fetched a garment bag from the hall and opened it.

"I don't have terribly many dresses that would fit both you and the occasion," she answered without acknowledging my thanks. "Only these two."

One of them was a black strapless number with a fitted bodice and a bell-skirt, and the other was wine red of some flowy material, with butterfly sleeves that fell over the shoulders, a loosely draping top, and a flowing skirt, with a narrow belt breaking the line at the waist. Both were tasteful. Both were also more expensive than anything I'd ever worn.

I loved them.

"I think I'd best try the red one. The other one would make me worry about a wardrobe malfunction the whole evening."

"But it clashes with your hair," Melissa said, dismayed. "I thought it would still be cherry red or I wouldn't have picked it."

"I'm going to wear a wig, so the color won't be a problem."

"And something to cover that bruise?" Travis asked dryly, but he looked concerned.

"I hope so."

I left Trevor and Jackson to brief them about why my face was such an interesting color and went to try the dress on. It was perfect. It brought out my curves while hiding the extra weight, and since I was shorter than Melissa, it came almost to my knees instead of mid-thigh, which could only be counted as a bonus.

"What do you think?" I asked when I returned to the living room, twirling a little to make the skirt billow nicely. I had the satisfaction of seeing both my brothers'—and Jackson's—eyes open wide in admiration.

"You look stunning," Trevor assured me. Jackson looked sort of confused.

Melissa didn't comment. She opened a large bag and took out a shoebox. "You'll need these with it."

She took the lid off the box to reveal a pair of black Christian Louboutin pumps, with their distinctive red soles and tasteful two-inch heels. I'd never had the courage to even touch one of those, let alone try them on. My mouth went dry.

"I think your feet are slightly bigger," I managed to say, while itching to grab the shoes.

"They're a size too small for me," she said with a shrug, as if owning a pair of expensive shoes she couldn't even wear wasn't a big deal. "I got them from a clearance sale once, just so a coworker of mine couldn't get them." Her smile was so satisfied I concluded there was no love lost between the women.

She gave the shoes to me and I held them with reverence. For a woman who didn't usually care how she looked, these shoes had really affected me. I placed them carefully on the floor and stepped into them. The leather was a little stiff, but the shoes were a perfect fit. I sighed in relief.

"I think they'll do," I said coolly, but then cracked a wide smile.

"Higher heels would look better with the dress," Melissa only said.

My outfit sorted, complete with a clutch and a pair of tasteful—and expensive—gemstone earrings Melissa also borrowed me, Travis and Melissa gathered the twins—to great protests from Mom and the children—

and left. While my parents were outside seeing them off, we took the opportunity to brief Trevor.

"It seems that the only thing the women have in common is the free medical services at the maternity clinic your mother works at," Jackson told him.

"Fuck. Mom's gonna be upset if someone from there turns out to be guilty. I'll ask Blair to get the list of their workers. That FBI contact of hers can run it against the names of known child traffickers."

"Did you learn anything at the playground?" I asked.

He shook his head. "Not many mothers were there, and those few were scared. The word's got around about the kidnappings. We talked mostly about general things, like how difficult it is to raise a child with no money. But no matter how hard, none of them would have given their child away."

"Had it been suggested to them?" I asked, instantly tense.

"Yes, and they weren't happy about it. Why?"

"Mom said Mrs. Morgan has been reprimanded a couple of times for forcefully advocating adoption to poor mothers."

Jackson and Trevor looked stunned. "Why didn't you say anything?" Jackson demanded.

"I don't know. I sort of forgot all about it." I fought not to blush when I remembered the conversation with Mom about getting pregnant by Jackson, which had wiped it from my mind. "Or maybe I dismissed her as an improbable suspect. Why would she kidnap her own grandson?"

Jackson looked aggravated. "Because she's made it clear that she doesn't find Melody a good enough mother. If she gives the babies to adoption so they'd have better families, she may have thought she was doing Robin a favor."

"Jackson's right," Trevor said. "She is the perfect suspect. She has access to all the mothers and their babies, knows their habits, has a motive, and since she's so interested in adoption, most likely the means too."

I felt sick. "But why wouldn't she do something when Robin died? She just abandoned him in the park?"

"I don't know. But who else had access to Melody's apartment? And if she had simply taken the child for a stroll while Melody slept, she probably would've reacted differently, taken the child to a hospital. But she was about to give the child away and wasn't thinking clearly. Or perhaps she couldn't admit being the one who had failed to look after the baby after all her criticism."

"So she's our prime suspect?"

"She's definitely the best person to start with. I'll call Blair and ask her to make a thorough background check and put Mrs. Morgan under surveillance."

"We could do that," I instantly suggested, but Jackson gave my shoulder a calming squeeze.

"We have another case to take care of tonight. So I suggest you go take a shower now, so we can be at the office in time for the makeup artist."

I wanted to protest. This was a far more important case. But we'd promised to help and we would. There were enough cops to keep an eye on one woman. Still, it was with reluctance I hadn't felt earlier that I headed to the shower.

Chapter Sixteen

CHRISTIAN, THE MAKEUP ARTIST, was a short and slender man in his fifties who was in raptures over my outfit and in horror over my face. "Never mind, I'll fix it."

But first he hid my hair with about a million hairpins under a nude skullcap he attached with some glue. The pins instantly began to press against my skull, but I didn't dare complain. Then he did my face. The bruise took forever to cover, but it did disappear completely. I wanted to know what he'd used, but he said it was a trade secret.

"Also, these are very expensive makeups."

I decided to let it be.

After he had finished, I didn't recognize my face. I didn't look exactly beautiful, but I did look striking—and strange, especially without hair. My eyes seemed larger and a bit slanted; my cheeks were leaner, my brows darker and heavier, and my lips plumper, with a lipstick that matched my dress. But if I didn't recognize my face, the chances were the thief wouldn't either.

"And now the wig. Would miss like to be blond or brunette? Short or long-haired?" He pulled out wig after wig from a large case. "All natural hair, of course."

"Dealer's choice," I said, unable to choose between the fine rugs.

"Brunette it is, then. I hear blondes have more fun, but this one complements your makeup and outfit."

I ended up with dark mahogany hair that reached below my shoulder blades in silky waves. I loved it as it was, but after gluing it in place, Christian spent an eternity creating a sophisticated chignon of it. It was so different from who I was, I felt perfectly sure even my mother wouldn't recognize me. Although that created a new worry.

"What if I can't pull off a woman this sophisticated?"

"I doubt anyone expects you to talk," Jackson said dryly. He was sitting behind his desk, taking care of some paperwork, but he'd kept a bemused eye on the proceedings the whole time.

"Gee, thanks."

"I'm just stating the realities. This isn't exactly the feminists' convention you're headed to. You're arm candy and that's good. No one will pay attention to you and you'll be able to observe unnoticed."

Christian inhaled sharply. "Not pay attention to such beauty? That's outrageous."

"Thanks," I said, blowing him a kiss.

Before I could slip into my dress again, we had to attach the wire on me. "It's best I hide it underneath your bra," Jackson said, coming to me with the mike and the transmitter cord that connected the two. "Good thing you're not wearing a plunging neckline, so we can hide this in your cleavage," he added with a grin, showing the tiny transmitter.

My heart skipping a few nervous beats, I stood perfectly still as he attached everything to their places with warm, sure hands, the mike ending up on my shoulder under the bra strap. His focus was unwaveringly on the task at hand, and he didn't even once try to cop a feel. I didn't know if I should be disappointed or relieved. But I couldn't help being embarrassed.

"You know, this is the closest a man has come to my breasts in years," I had to say to hide the confusion his hands on my body caused. He grinned.

"Pity this is all you're getting."

"This is plenty after such a long time." But I let out a silent sigh of relief when he finished and I could put on my dress. We checked that nothing was showing and that everything was glued to their places and operating perfectly.

The detectives arrived with Westley. The first two were in their rumpled, cheap suits, but Westley was wearing an expensive black-tie number by some famous designer. It didn't make him look like James Bond, exactly, but I wouldn't mind showing up with him at the party. I gave him an appreciative once-over that made Jackson raise his brows, amused.

All three stopped when they saw me and staggered. Then, as one, they leaned forward to take a closer look, and amazed smiles spread on their faces, all of this happening so in sync it made me roll my eyes.

"You look great," Pete said to me, and then gave the makeup artist still packing his things an appreciative nod. "You've outdone yourself this time, Christian." The man beamed.

"I must say, Miss Hayes, that your transformation is staggering," Westley said, studying me with much greater interest than I had checked him out earlier. "Not that you weren't perfectly attractive before," he hastened to assure me. "Just perhaps not quite ... at the level of the people at the party."

I wasn't offended ... much. "I borrowed everything from my brother's wife."

"And who might he be?"

Figures he'd be more interested in Travis.

"Travis Hayes, Assistant DA at the Brooklyn Public Defender Service."

"Of course! I went to Harvard with him."

Of course he did. But had he worked his way through it like Travis, or had his parents paid everything? I only smiled though, which he interpreted to mean delight for the shared acquaintance. I could also see that my estimate rose in his eyes. A sister of an assistant DA was much better than an apprentice P.I.

"What should I call you tonight?" he asked.

"Henrietta Fern," I stated promptly to a chorus of gleeful snorts. "What? It's a good name."

"It's also the one you used as a waitress in Mr. Westley's party."

"Yes, but I didn't get to tell it to anyone."

"How about your second name and your mother's maiden name," Jackson suggested sensibly.

"I don't look like Katherine O'Malley," I said, miffed.

"Yes, you do. More to the point, you'll be able to remember it."

"It's a beautiful name," Westley assured me.

"Can you at least call me Kate?"

"Absolutely. And you'll call me Thom."

Pete rubbed his hands together. "Great. Does everyone know their roles?"

Thom nodded. "I'm to be me with a new date I'll show around—and then ignore so that she has a chance to mingle and look around."

"And what will you do if you spot your man?" Pete asked me.

"Inform you and don't try to take him alone," I answered dutifully.

"Promise?" Jackson said with a smile.

"I learned my lesson the first time."

With that, we filed out of the office and into two cars that were waiting by the street. Jackson went with the detectives in their car. Thom and I got into a black Town Car with a driver. "I hired him for the drive over, but we'll return by taxi, as we won't know how long we'll be."

"Very classy. I haven't had a chauffeured vehicle since we hired a limo to our prom with my friends." That hadn't ended well. Two of the girls drank too much and threw up in the car, and the driver became angry and made us pay for the cleanup. But I wasn't about to drink anything tonight.

"Champagne?" Thom said just then, reaching for a cabinet in the middle between us and the driver.

I snorted out a laugh, remembering the woman from his party who hadn't been happy with the beverages. "Who was the loud woman who lost her emerald necklace?" I asked, refusing the drink, though I sorely needed it to calm my nerves.

"Mrs. Winston-Smith, an insanely wealthy widow of an industrialist, and a patron of numerous charities. I invited her because everyone invites her. I don't know why she attended. Probably because I promised money to her favorite charity."

An eye-opening insight into the lives of these people.

Our destination was on Manhattan, which I hadn't expected. We drove across the Brooklyn Bridge fairly painlessly and headed south towards Battery Park, to one of the newer skyscrapers by it. "We'll be unfashionably early, but our friends deemed it was best."

I nodded, smiling inwardly to his attempt to avoid the word police. We'd agreed not to talk about our mission, as you never knew who might be listening—the driver in this case.

The car pulled over by the main entrance and the driver got out to open the door for us. Thom exchanged a few words with him, probably about the payment, and escorted me in. The building didn't have a liveried doorman. Instead, it had a security desk and a sharp-looking man in a suit wearing an ear-piece sitting behind it. Thom presented his invitation and the guy rounded the desk to us and promptly searched him for weapons.

My heartbeat accelerated painfully when he turned to me. What if he found the wire? But Jackson had done a good job hiding it, and at any rate, the guy didn't go too near to my breasts before asking for my clutch and taking a peek in. I only had a lipstick, my phone, and some cash in there, and he handed it back without showing any interest.

Another couple, an older gentleman and his wife, entered the lobby just as we were given permission to approach the elevators—the guard's words—and were given the same treatment, much to the lady's dismay.

She was still complaining about it when they entered the elevator car with us.

The man ignored her and just offered Thom his hand and introduced himself. He paid no attention to me, and Thom didn't introduce me either. I knew this was how most of the evening would go, but even though I knew my role, it still aggravated me to be so overlooked. So I nodded at the wife. She nodded back but didn't offer her name.

The ride to the twenty-fifth floor was long, even though the elevator was fast, and the higher we rose the more nervous I got. I caught my reflection in the mirror and almost jumped in fright, thinking there was a stranger in the car with us, before I remembered it was me. I wanted to test the mike, but didn't dare touch it with people present. And anyway, I didn't have an earpiece of my own and wouldn't know if it didn't work. I just had to trust that Jackson and the detectives had everything under control at the other end.

Finally, the elevator pinged to signal our arrival and the doors opened straight into the apartment. I drew in a steadying breath and followed Thom out. It was show time.

Chapter Seventeen

THE ENTIRE FLOOR BELONGED TO OUR HOST, Todd Baxter. His name didn't mean anything to me, and even after Thom briefed me about him on our way over, I still didn't really understand what he did, except money.

"That's how it is with most of the people you'll meet here, apart from the hangers-on. They haven't had to create anything, innovate, start from the ground up," Thom said, sounding a bit contemptuous. He'd done all three. "He just makes money with other people's money."

And he did it well, judging by the size of the place, only a fraction of which was open to his guests. The view alone, which opened from the floor-to-ceiling windows towards Battery Park and over Hudson, cost more than I could dream of making in my life. After the squalor of the slums where I'd spent my day, this place and the people in their party finest felt surreal, almost ... obscene. But I had a job to do, so I stiffened my spine and put a smile on my face.

The room was decorated with subdued, impersonal colors and expensive designer furniture; it had space for several large seating areas, a fireplace big enough to roast a pig in—not that anyone would in a place this tasteful—and a long dining table for twenty people at one end, which for the party had been set for the buffet. Judging by the amount of food on it, I wouldn't go hungry tonight.

Provided I was allowed to eat.

I eyed the women already present in dismay. All were tall, so thin they would disappear if they turned to their profile, and had perfect hair and makeup. They were wearing a variation of the same skimpy dress, and their heels were so high I got vertigo just looking at them.

"What is this, a supermodel convention?" I asked Thom in a low voice. He grinned.

"Hosts of these parties often hire models for the evening to add beauty to the selection of guests." Great. "But it's good you don't look like them. People will believe you're my genuine date."

Double great.

"I'm not threatened by those women. I grew up with a supermodel."

His eyes got the dreamy glaze men always did when they thought of my sister. "Ah, Theresa... Is she still single?"

"I'm afraid not." I saw no reason to tell him he would

be the wrong gender for her even if she had still been single.

"That's my luck. When I'm finally wealthy enough to attract the women I was nuts about when I was younger, they're already taken."

"I'm sure you don't need money to attract women," I said, slightly distracted, scanning the guests as we made our way to the host. Despite Thom's fears that we'd be the only ones here this early, there were plenty of people present already and the circle around the host was thick.

"Do you really think so?" he asked, delighted. I'd already forgotten what I'd said, but I nodded.

"Absolutely." He pulled straighter and checked out the models with renewed interest. I grinned. "But perhaps not tonight?"

He smiled too. "Perhaps."

"Or at least wait until I've ... gone to my own way." I saw no reason why he couldn't have fun tonight. He agreed readily to that.

Female-to-male ratio favored the men on the prowl this early in the evening because of the hired guests. And as the vast room was open-plan, I'd soon checked out all the men that looked even remotely like they could be our guy. It wasn't terribly difficult, as the party didn't have as many sport stars present with their muscled bodies as Thom's had. Then I checked the rest of the men too, just in case he'd gone through a transformation rivalling my own.

"No one here yet," I muttered, seemingly to myself, but actually for the benefit of those listening at the other end of the mike.

"Of course not," a woman said behind me. "The really important people won't arrive until much later."

I smiled at the forty-something woman who looked vaguely artistic, like an author or an art critic with short, electric-blue hair and a black, cape-like dress that reached her ankles. Her fingers were covered in rings, and I actually expected her to whip out a long cigarette holder any moment.

"Shorter lines to the food, then," I quipped.

"Gad, yes. No one eats free food like the rich and famous," she said with an exaggerated roll of her heavily made-up eyes, and then offered me her hand. "Gloria Killough." I took her hand and then choked, temporarily forgetting the name I was supposed to use, but luckily she interpreted it the way she wanted.

"Yes, *that* Gloria Killough, from *the* New York Times."

I smiled, as if I'd recognized her. "Kate O'Malley."

"A fellow Irishwoman?" Her phony accent was horrible, but I nodded.

"Fourth generation American though."

"Whereabouts in Ireland do you come from? My family is from Killough originally, natch."

I racked my brain to remember where Mom's family

originated. I hadn't expected this fake persona to need such an extensive backstory. "Somewhere near Cork," I winged it, hoping Killough wasn't anywhere near there or she would start comparing family connections.

"Ever been there?"

"I haven't had the ... chance." Money was what I meant, but my character could probably afford to vacation in Europe.

"Didn't you take a year off after college?"

"Yes, but I went on a tour with a band." It was true too, though I'd actually dropped out of college for it. It was my ex-husband's now former band and they hadn't been famous. Far from it.

She perked. "You were a groupie? Which band? What was it like? Tell me everything."

I was saved by Thom, who had managed to catch the attention of our host, a man in his fifties with a deep tan from either tennis or sailing—or both—judging by the lines around his eyes from squinting in the sun, and his callused palm, which I got a feel of when he shook my hand. Since he could afford to have them manicured, I took them to mean he was proud of his hobby. The handshake was firm and his straight gaze was oh-so-honest. I'd trust him with my money.

"Where do you find such beautiful women, Thom?" he said with an appreciative smile to me. I smiled back. Thom blinked, unable to come up with a story. We clearly should've thought about the backstory more carefully, but I hadn't expected this much interest.

I rushed to his rescue. I leaned closer to Baxter, as if divulging a great secret: "I actually crashed his party the other day."

He burst out laughing. "That was bold of you. But you couldn't have managed the same here."

"I did admire your security," I flattered him shamelessly.

"One can never be too careful."

"Exactly. I mean, poor Thom's party ended in chaos when this horrible man robbed everyone blind."

"I heard about it. Did you lose anything?"

"Luckily no. I was … otherwise engaged at the time." I shot a coy glance at Thom, hoping he would look suitably smug, as if we'd been making out at the time of the robbery. He didn't catch my cue, but our host didn't notice.

"Well, worry not. No one's going to rob you here."

"I feel so safe."

Our minute with the host up, we walked on, shaking hands with whomever Thom knew or wanted to know. I was introduced to everyone, but no one was interested in my life story.

"Let's head to the buffet," I said to Thom.

"Are you hungry? I should've taken you to dinner before the party." He sounded contrite.

"This is not a date, you know. Besides, it's easier to engage people over selecting food. Were any of those people at your party?" I asked, nodding at the people milling around the table.

He paled. "I hope no one from my party shows up. That was a disaster. Why did you bring it up?"

"Just gauging people's reactions. If the man wasn't invited, he may have been someone's plus one."

"That would mean we'd have to keep an eye on the women too?" He sounded hopeful.

"Or men, I'm not judging."

His shoulders slumped. "Well, let's get something to eat and then we can mingle."

"Or you can abandon me here and enjoy the party." It took some reassuring, but finally he left to find his friends, leaving me to do my job.

Whoever Baxter's caterer was, they were great. The food was tastefully and logically displayed—as a former waiter I knew how important logical layout was to keeping the line moving. The selection was good, and easy to eat without it spilling all over the place—or your dress. I'd catered the latter kind of spreads too— disasters one and all. And critically for my mission, it took long enough to round the table to have a couple of conversations while queuing.

And thanks to my upgraded looks, I didn't even have to start the conversations.

"I haven't seen you around before," a man about my age drawled. He was well-groomed, well-dressed and well-drunk. Everything about him screamed a trust-fund slacker and I disliked him on principle. But perhaps Kate would be more accepting.

I flashed him a smile. "That's because I haven't been around before."

"Where did Westley find you, then?"

"Brooklyn."

He grinned. "I haven't been across the bridge all that much."

"You're missing a lot."

"Evidently." Then one of the hired guests caught his eye, and he prowled—or stumbled more like—to her direction offering me an escape. I tried not to feel miffed that he'd dumped me so fast.

Next man to address me was twice my age and he didn't carry his years well. He was grossly overweight and the color on his face wasn't healthy. Judging by the amount of food he heaped on his plate, he was looking at a cardiac arrest in his very near future. That didn't stop him from making a move on me.

"When Westley tires of you, give me a call."

I gave him a slow look. "I don't think so."

His face turned purple. "Look, missy, when a woman is invited by me, she doesn't refuse if she knows what's what."

"I guess I don't know, then." This time I was the one to move, skipping a couple of people in the line before me—and missing a treat I'd been looking forward to in the process, which made me even more annoyed with the man.

So far, the buffet hadn't worked the way I'd hoped.

"Were you at Thom's party the other night?"

My heart jumped at the question made by the woman I'd overtaken. She didn't look annoyed—or like she'd recognized me as a waitress there, which I'd feared. Incidentally, I lived in constant dread that the snobby Mrs. Winston-Smith would make an appearance here. So far, so good.

"Yes. You?"

She shuddered. "Yes. Was anything of yours stolen?"

"No, I only had these earrings worth anything to steal, and they're not easy to remove unnoticed. You?"

"Yes, a bracelet. I have no idea how it happened. Must have been in that chaos when we were exiting."

I tried to think back to it, but the memory I had was of the man rounding the exiting throng from behind, as if he hadn't even been near it. "Must be," was all I said. "All that water, people pushing each other out of the way. Anything could've happened there."

"Do you think he'll return tonight?"

"With the security they have in this building? I don't think so." I tried to sound relieved, but I worried that this charade would be for nothing.

"I hope you're right."

With my plate full, I retired to a quiet spot to eat and observe the guests. The place was starting to fill up, making my task more difficult. It didn't help that every man wore the same outfit and pretty much the same haircut too. Individuality was frowned upon in these circles. I needed a better lookout spot.

I made to move when a man spoke behind me. "Tracy?"

Chapter Eighteen

MY HEART STOPPED COMPLETELY, and only that prevented me from reacting. I took a sip of my glass of wine to regain my composure, my hand shaking only lightly. I felt him lean over my shoulder and got a whiff of his delicious scent, unobtrusive and sexy as hell. My sorely-neglected lady parts took instant notice.

"Undercover, huh?" the deep voice drawled.

I pulled back to give him a cool look of the sort I was sure Kate would give. "Do we know each other?"

We did, of course. Jonny Moreira. He and I had bumped into each other more often than it was acceptable for a mafia enforcer and a P.I., but I hadn't expected to see him here. He was a henchman of Craig Douglas, and even though mafia and money went together, they never did it quite this publicly.

He was in his early thirties, and around six-foot-three of intimidating muscle poured into a tailor-made suit. His black hair was combed back. His angular face was hard, and his deep-set brown eyes never stopped scanning his surroundings for danger.

Except now they were giving me an amused once-over. "Apparently not." He had the audacity to wink. Then he offered me his hand. "Jonny Moreira."

"Kate O'Malley."

He was trying so hard not to laugh that deep crinkles appeared around his eyes. "And what is it that you do for a living, Kate?"

He was actually the first person to ask that. "I'm a consultant." It was vague enough, and in certain circumstances even true.

"And what do you consult about?"

"Everything."

"I bet you're good at it."

"The best." He laughed aloud at that. "And what is it that you do, Mr. Moreira?" I was beginning to enjoy this conversation.

"I'm a businessman."

"And what's your business?"

"Transportation."

That was as close to the truth as he'd get. "And what brings you here tonight?"

"Baxter is my funds manager."

"And here I thought he had such reliable eyes."

He grinned. "I know."

I picked up my glass again and scanned the people over its rim. He studied them too, but with less subtlety.

"You know, for a businessman you're awfully … alert." I couldn't see his boss anywhere, so it couldn't be for him that he was being vigilant.

"And for a consultant you're very curious."

"It's my best quality."

"So who are we looking for?"

"I don't know what you're talking about," I said primly. "But since you're interested in these people anyway, you might look for a man in his late thirties, medium height, strong build, and light brown hair thinning at the top."

"The guy who robbed Thom's place?"

"How the fuck do you know about that?" He hadn't been at the party. I would've noticed him.

"Thom told me."

I'd forgotten the two of them knew each other. "He should be more careful with who he trusts."

"He actually believes I am who I say I am."

"Do you have businesses together?"

"Nothing that would interest your friends at the other end of that mike you're wearing."

"I'm not wearing anything." But I couldn't help glancing at my shoulder to see if my dress had slipped.

Moreira sneered. "Gotcha."

"Piss off."

"Now is that any way for a lady to talk?"

"I'm not a lady, I'm Irish."

His deep laugh attracted the attention of quite a few women around us. Looks-wise, he was worth the attention. Pity about the rest of him. Not that he would give me the time of day in normal circumstances.

"Why don't we mingle a little?" he suggested.

"I thought I'd set up shop somewhere with a good view so I don't miss anyone."

"That would make it look like you're sulking in the corner and draw attention to you."

"Well, I'm obviously being grossly neglected by my date and I don't know anyone, so sulking is a perfectly plausible course of action."

"Come on, you didn't doll up to stand in a corner, did you?"

I did not. I put away my plate, took my wine glass, and followed him deeper into the party. It was a vastly different experience than with Thom. Whether for his size, his actual job, or his standing among these people based on some imagined position, everyone paused when he approached, eager to shake hands with him. And when he introduced me—as Kate O'Malley, consultant—people actually took notice of me. It was weird to have their attention, heady and frightening. I almost forgot what I was here for in my eagerness to not embarrass myself.

"So you upgraded from Thom already, you sly girl," Gloria Killough said, having appeared next to me as I waited for Moreira to finish his conversation.

I fought not to blush. "No, I ... know Moreira of old."

"Really? I've been dying to get my hands on someone who knows him. Would you be willing to talk on record?"

"I thought you were an art critic."

"Yes, well, I'm not above scoops. So how about it?"

I didn't have to think twice. Not that I owed him loyalty, but you didn't blab on mafia and live to tell the tale. Besides, she likely didn't know who he actually was and I had no idea who she thought she'd be getting the scoop on. "I'm sorry, I have nothing to tell."

"That's what all his women say. What is it that keeps them so loyal to him? Is he great in bed? I bet he is."

This time I did blush. "I wouldn't know."

Moreira noticed us talking and his affable demeanor turned cold, making him more resemble the scary henchman I'd first met. He didn't say anything; he just led me away, as if I hadn't been in the middle of a conversation. If I'd wanted to stay, his highhanded behavior would've aggravated me.

"So who are you to attract the attention of the New York Times?"

He cocked a brow, but it wasn't amused. "You know exactly who I am."

"Okay, who do these people think you are, then?"

A slow smile spread on his face. "Someone more savory. Now, where do you want to head next?"

We'd circled the whole room, but it was so full of people, all I could see was a sea of black backs and shoulders. "I need a better lookout spot."

"How about near the bar? Everyone's bound to head there."

Now why didn't I think of that? "Excellent idea. Lead the way."

He took my glass that still had some wine in it and put it on the tray of a waiter walking by. Then he headed to the bar and I followed, keeping close to his back to make the most of the path he opened.

There was quite a throng around the bar. Two young men were pouring drinks as fast as they could and still it wasn't fast enough. I scoped them out, but neither of them was my man. People lining the bar had their backs turned to me, but I felt confident I'd had a good look at the thief's backside, and none of these men had quite the shoulders he did.

"He's not here."

"Don't give up so fast. He might show up."

"I don't think he will. Didn't you see the security downstairs?"

"They can be persuaded to look the other way." He flicked the lapel of his jacket open, giving me a peek at his trimmed torso—and the gun in its holster.

"How the hell did you get that in here?" I hissed at him, but he just grinned.

"I'm in the security business."

"You're a frickin' mafia enforcer. That's hardly the same."

"You say tomato, I say lax security."

"I don't like the sound of that."

"Relax. I doubt he'll do such a brazen robbery twice in a row. He's much more likely to try for the safe. And there are men waiting for him there."

"The police?" He gave me a slow look. "I guess not."

"What would you like to drink?" he said, changing the topic.

"I'd best stick to red wine."

Moreira headed into the throng at the bar, people parting from his way gratifyingly fast. I scanned the crowd again, but saw nothing.

"This is impossible," I muttered aloud for the benefit of the mike. "I think Moreira is right and the guy will go for the safe if he's here."

I had no way of knowing if Jackson and the detectives even heard me, which made me feel alone all of a sudden. What if the communications didn't work and something did happen?

I took a deep breath and pushed the queasy sensation away. I had to act as if everything was working perfectly. And if I assumed Moreira was right, I'd better head in the direction of the safe.

"If I were a study, where would I be?" I muttered to

myself, but a man passing by heard me and grinned.

"I didn't take you for someone who'd be interested in books."

"Because you know me so well?"

"No, because you're so beautiful."

Pleasure fought with annoyance, but the latter won. "Congratulations, that's the most sexist thing anyone has said to me the whole evening."

The man had the good sense to blush. "I thought women like to be called beautiful."

"But they don't like to be called stupid."

"Right … so are you here with someone?"

"Me."

The man blanched when Moreira spoke behind him, and moved on without a word.

"That was fun," I said to Moreira.

"I could tell by your face you were enjoying yourself immensely," he said dryly, making me sigh.

"This isn't working. All I'm getting is being hit on by assholes."

"Thanks."

I smiled, taking a glass he gave me. "You weren't trying to pick me up, you were trying to annoy me." He shrugged as if the two were the same. "I think I should go check out the safe. Nothing's going to happen here."

I'd barely finished the sentence when all the lights went off, plunging the room into darkness.

Chapter Nineteen

I WAS INSTANTLY PRESSED TO THE FLOOR by a strong hand on my neck. I would've shrieked in fright, but I recognized Moreira's scent. Trust him to act like a bodyguard.

"Close your eyes," he ordered me.

"Why?"

"You'll get your night vision back."

Since that would be handy, I obeyed. Above me, people were starting to mill about after the initial startled pause, and voices were being raised, both frightened and angry.

"I'll get trampled down here if we don't move," I said to Moreira, who was still holding his hand on my neck.

"Okay, open your eyes. Can you see?"

With my night vision activated, there was plenty of ambient light coming through the windows at the other end of the room for me to detect the forms of people and furniture around me. I put the miraculously upright wine glass on the nearest surface.

"Yes."

"Good. Keep low and let's head towards the kitchen."

"Shouldn't we try to find the thief?" I'd eat my wig if this was an accidental power-outage.

"You couldn't find him even with the lights on," he reminded me. "But he has to escape somehow and he can't use the elevator while the power's cut. We'll wait for him at the back door."

With his hand guiding me from the back, we made our way surprisingly painlessly through the crowd in the direction of the kitchen. It helped that everyone else was moving towards the windows, calling for someone to do something—anyone but them. A few enterprising souls had taken out their cellphones and were using them as flashlights, destroying what little night vision they had left. I could only hope it would mess with the thief's eyesight too.

"Do you think he's robbing the guests now?" I asked Moreira in a low voice.

"Why else would he have cut the power?"

"To escape in the chaos after already stealing something?" I was pretty sure he'd done just that at Thom's.

"He wouldn't draw attention to himself if that was the case."

That was true too, though I wasn't ready to give up my theory either.

"Maybe he stole something large from the safe and

needs the darkness to hide it."

"The room's secured."

"By your men or those who let you bring in your weapon?"

"Neither, but they're reliable."

"What if he's incapacitated them?" I thought it was perfectly plausible, but he gave a derisive snort.

"Four sturdy men?"

"Maybe he used tranquilizer gas."

"This isn't a heist movie." But he changed direction to head deeper into the apartment, keeping close to the wall. "You guard the kitchen door."

The last thing I wanted was to be left alone in the dark, facing the thief, so I hastened after him. "The hell I am. He almost killed me the last time."

"What?" His angry question was a barely audible growl.

My heart skipped a frightened—or appreciative— beat. "Never mind. I was exaggerating. Keep moving."

It was pitch black in the hallway, but somehow Moreira seemed to be able to see. I might as well have been walking with my eyes closed, so I kept my hand on his back to follow his movements. I wasn't copping a feel. Honest.

He turned to the left and paused almost immediately at what I presumed was a door. I heard him draw his weapon. "Wait here."

This time I didn't argue.

I more felt than heard him move away, the warmth of his body disappearing, leaving me to shiver in the hallway. His scent lingered. I leaned my shoulder against the wall to have a fixed point in the darkness. I strained my ears to hear something, but if there were people with him in the room, they were silent.

I didn't like the sound—or non-sound—of that.

Should I call for help?

I wasn't given a chance.

A large, gloved hand pressed over my face from behind, pulling my head tightly against a hard chest. I almost wet myself in fright and I tried to inhale sharply, but the hand covered my mouth and nose, cutting off the air completely. I began to struggle, but he wrapped his other arm around me and held me painfully fast.

"Don't make a sound and I'll let you breathe."

The voice was little more than a whisper by my ear, flat and devoid of any personal tone that would've helped me to recognize it. I was panicking already for fear that I would suffocate, but I forced my body to relax. The hand moved off my nose and I drew in a desperate breath, the nose not getting the job done fast enough. My head was spinning.

"Let's move, quietly." He began to pull me backwards and I struggled in my heels to keep up. One of my shoes fell off and landed on the hardwood floor with a clunk.

"It's only the work of a moment to break your neck the way I'm holding you, if you do that again."

Tears of terror flooded my eyes, nearly blocking my nose again. My heart was thumping in my throat as I limped backwards with only one heel, desperate to keep the remaining shoe on. I lost my clutch at some point, but it didn't make any sound as it dropped from my limp fingers and the man didn't notice. Or at least I wasn't punished for it.

I had no idea what direction he was taking me, or how long it took to reach there, but he moved with such surety that he had to be wearing night-vision goggles. I couldn't see anything in the dark or hear anything but his breathing by my ear. I feared I would faint for the lack of oxygen and I fought not to give in to it. I'd been unconscious in front of this man once. I wouldn't be again.

He reached a door and had to remove the arm around me to open it, but the other took a tighter hold of my face, his elbow digging sharply in my chest. I couldn't escape. But I took the opportunity to silently remove the remaining shoe, to make it easier for me to move in case he dragged me much farther.

We went through the door with our backs first and it closed again with a quiet click, indicating it had locked. It was dark there too, but I was surrounded by cooler air that reminded me of stairwells.

Before I could properly register this, the man released me. It was so sudden I dropped on my bottom, gasping for breath, acutely in pain. As if from a distance, I heard his retreating steps.

I wanted to lie there, panting, and never get up, but I refused to be cowed. Summoning the last of my strength, I pushed myself up, using the wall for support. My legs were shaking, but they held. I was wondering what I should do next when the lights flooded back on. The power cut was over.

I blinked to adjust my eyes to the brightness and took in my surroundings. I was outside the apartment in a bland, short hallway that led to stairs. The man was nowhere to be seen. I hadn't expected him to be.

"The thief is in the back stairs," I said in the mike. "Do you hear me? The back stairs. I'm in pursuit."

Frustrated for not knowing if I had backup or not, I took off after the man. This was the last time I'd wear a wire without a chance to hear from the other end.

The stairs led both up and down, but I had to make a fast decision, so I headed down. The man had a good head start, but he couldn't get out of the stairwell, as the only exits were to the apartments, and their back doors would surely be locked. The stairs circled the elevator shaft, so I couldn't see him or hear him ahead of me, but I didn't let that slow me down. And I refused to think that there were twenty-five floors to descend before I'd reach the street. It would be as many floors for him and he might tire too.

Unless he happened to catch the elevator.

"Fuck!" I said, grounding to a halt when the unmistakable sound of a moving elevator car came through the wall. "He's in the elevator," I said to the mike.

There was no point in continuing my pursuit, so I stopped by the elevator door to read the display. "He's definitely heading down." But then I heard someone running down the stairs above me. "Hang on, someone's coming."

I tensed, listening to the fast-approaching steps, and shrieked in fright when Moreira rounded the corner and almost collided with me. He took a hold of my shoulders to prevent me from falling. Then he pulled me against him and kissed me for all he was worth.

"Don't ever disappear like that," he said when he released me. My head was spinning and I had to steady myself against the elevator door. That had been some kiss. Then my eyes focused and registered the display again. "He's heading to the garage," I said to the mike, slightly out of breath.

"Are you all right? What happened?" Moreira asked. "The lights came back on and you weren't there. I found a shoe, and a bag. Then another shoe." He had the items in his hands and he gave them to me. I put the shoes back on, grateful to have everything back. I didn't want to upset Melissa by losing them.

"The thief abducted me and now he's getting away."

"What do you mean, abducted?" he demanded.

I told him what had happened, to his increasing anger that didn't promise anything good for the thief if he found him before the police did.

"I'm glad you're okay," he only said though when I finished. "Come, let's head back up."

Chapter Twenty

THE BACK DOOR TO BAXTER'S APARTMENT was locked, but it was a moment's work for Moreira to pick it, as if the state of the art lock was just a fleeting nuisance. I secretly admired his skill with the picks, and was determined to learn to be as good as he was. I even had my own set of picks he'd given me as a really weird gift.

The door opened to a short, dimly-lit hallway that was nowhere near the kitchen. Moreira led me through the apartment and we soon reached the living area, where the party was back on as if nothing had happened.

"Apparently it takes more than a power cut to ruin a party," I said dryly.

"Nothing was stolen from the guests, so they think it was just a glitch. He emptied the safe, and even the host doesn't know about it yet."

"That's about to change." I nodded towards the apartment elevator where the detectives were exiting. And behind them, Jackson. Tears of relief sprang to my eyes.

Moreira sneered. "You go to your boss." And he disappeared before I had a chance to thank him.

I could see Jackson was searching for me over the heads of the crowd, but since I couldn't greet him publicly, I spoke to the mike: "I'm behind you on the other side of the hallway."

He headed instantly towards me through the crowd, leaving the host to the detectives, and soon reached me. He pulled me into a tight embrace, and for the second time that night I was thoroughly kissed. This time I wasn't so startled I couldn't have enjoyed it when it happened. I was flustered when he released me.

"Come, let's get you home. You can talk to the detectives tomorrow."

Wordlessly, exhausted beyond belief now that I was safe, I followed him to the elevator. The face of a strange woman met me at the mirror there and it took me longer this time to remember that it was me. My makeup was still flawless, a testament to Christian's skill, but my hair had come lose from its chignon—although the wig was perfectly in place. But there was something wrong with the image and it took me the whole ride down to realize what it was.

"The bastard stole my earrings!"

I SLEPT LATER THAN I'D INTENDED, and I was still exhausted when I shuffled to the kitchen around noon. Jarod had bought donuts and since they were still warm, I deduced with my mad detective skills it hadn't been long since he'd purchased them. He wasn't in the apartment and he hadn't left a note, but he only ever left home for work or—if forced—university, so I wasn't worried.

I'd slept with the wig and makeup on, so I spent the next hour removing them. The hairpins had burrowed into my scalp, and the layers of makeup seemed impervious to all my removal tonics. A long shower removed what was left of the signs of the previous night, and when I was done, a pale face with a yellowish bruise stared at me in the mirror. I should've kept the makeup on. It would probably have survived the shower.

I'd barely got my clothes on and the bruise concealed when Jackson arrived with a large coffee and muffins, but without Misty, who he'd left with a neighbor. Though I'd already eaten the donuts, I almost teared up at the sight.

"How are you doing this morning," he asked, concerned. I lifted the coffee cup.

"Brilliantly now that I have this." I flashed him a smile, but he looked awkward. "What is it?"

He cleared his throat. "About the kiss last night…"

I'd forgotten all about being kissed—twice! You'd think a woman with a dry spell that had lasted over half a decade would remember such toe-curling, blood-heating occasions, especially with two such attractive men. But no. I couldn't tell that to Jackson though.

"It was sorely needed and well-appreciated, but if you fear I'm going to sue you for sexual harassment or something, I absolutely will not."

His smile wasn't as relieved as I'd have thought. "That's good, but I can assure you it won't happen again. It was the occasion, and because you didn't look like yourself."

That showed me. "Don't worry, I'm not upset about it. Now, what's the plan for the day?"

"It's Sunday. You could take a day off, you know."

"But we have a kidnapper to catch, and a thief." The guy had managed to escape despite the detectives heeding the instructions I'd given through the mike. At least the damn thing had been operational. "What did he steal anyway?"

"We don't know yet. Baxter wouldn't tell."

"Well, it couldn't have been anything large." Jackson gave me a questioning look, so I explained my theory about why he'd cut the power. "But he wasn't carrying anything when he took me."

Jackson's fury was a sight to behold when he thought of my abduction. "I'm fucking crucifying this guy."

I patted his shoulder. "We'll have to find him first."

"I don't understand why he took you. It was dark. He could've just snuck away."

"Maybe he saw Moreira and thought he needed me as a shield."

"Probably. Let's go talk with the detectives."

Detectives Newman and Migliaccio looked like they'd slept in their suits, or hadn't slept at all. "What the fuck happened last night?" Pete demanded to know. "And where the fuck did Moreira go?"

"I think he's allergic to the police," I said dryly.

"Fuck his sensitivities. We need to talk with him. He went into the study before we got to the scene. Where can we find him?"

"I have no idea. I've never had to contact him."

"But you two clearly knew each other well."

I blushed when I realized they'd heard everything we'd talked about. "Not that well."

"Do you think he's in league with the thief?"

"I ... hadn't thought of it." I hated how my stomach fell at the notion. He was a criminal, for crying out loud. "The thief has to have some accomplices. But Moreira wasn't at Thom's party, and he was with me when the lights went off."

"Are you sure he wasn't the guy who abducted you?"

"Yes." Of this I had no doubt.

"Why? It was dark."

"He was shorter, for one, and he didn't smell like anything."

"Smell?"

"Moreira was wearing this amazing scent. He couldn't have got rid of it so fast."

To my surprise, the men actually believed me. I gave the detectives a thorough report, including Moreira's assessment about the security. "And there were no cameras at the back door, so the thief could've just got in through there."

"It was locked," Migliaccio said.

"It took Moreira twenty seconds to pick it." Then another thought hit. "What if the thief never left?"

"What do you mean?" Pete demanded.

"Well, did you actually see him leave?"

"No, but we're going through the security footage from the garage. He's bound to show up in it."

"Unless he returned to the party."

All three gave me disbelieving looks. "How?" Jackson demanded.

"I couldn't see anything in the dark hallway. I simply assumed he ran down the stairs, but what if he went up? Sent the elevator to the garage, ensuring you'd head there, and returned to the party when the coast was clear."

"Fuck. We'll have to go through the footage of the people leaving the party too."

"That still doesn't explain why he cut the power," Jackson reminded us.

Pete shrugged. "Until we know more, I'll assume that the alarm on the safe was connected to the main powerline."

"That's stupid."

"People aren't always clever about their security."

"Has he blacked-out the entire party before?" I asked.

"No, this was the first. Maybe other safes could be accessed without it."

"Or maybe we're dealing with a different guy."

Pete groaned. "I hope the fuck not."

We left the detectives to their work. We had our own case to solve. We headed to the hospital, just in time to witness Melody arguing with her doctor about going home.

"I can't stay here anymore, I'll go crazy," she pleaded.

"Wouldn't you rather rest here where people can look after you?" I asked her. I wouldn't let a mother who'd just lost a baby stay home alone.

She started crying. "I don't deserve to be looked after." I put an arm around her and held her close. I wasn't much of a hugger, but we all have to step out of our comfort zones occasionally.

"Of course you do."

"I couldn't even look after my child. I should've given him away like my mother said. Then he would be alive."

I wanted to wring her mother's neck for her cruelty. "You know he died of natural causes. That might have happened no matter who was taking care of him."

"Just let me go home where I can be with what I have left of him."

I glanced at the doctor, who gave a reluctant nod. "But I'd rather she wasn't alone," he said.

"Perhaps we could call your mother," the nurse suggested. "Where is she today?"

That was the million dollar question. Trevor had called earlier and told us the woman had disappeared, and hadn't been seen since the previous afternoon.

"There's nothing shady in her finances," he'd told us. "No sudden influx of money. If she steals the babies for adoption, she's not profiting from it."

"So you're saying she isn't our woman?" Jackson had asked.

"I'm not saying anything until I've exhausted all lines of inquiry." So we'd come to the hospital with the hopes that she would visit her daughter.

"Mom has her charities on weekends," Melody said, sounding bitter. "Our Lady's orphanage on Saturdays, and Holy Cross's Church on Sundays. Food kitchen. Helping everyone but her grandson."

That explained her bitter tone. "Maybe she could make an exception today?"

"I don't want her. I'll ask Mrs. Paige."

I decided not to tell her that her neighbor might not be home yet and just helped her to get dressed, while Jackson left the room to make a call to Trevor. I itched to go hunt for Mrs. Morgan, but instead we gave Melody a ride home.

Chapter Twenty-one

I WAS EXHAUSTED IN A DIFFERENT WAY by the time we'd returned Melody to her home and made sure Mrs. Paige was there to look after her. Mrs. Paige only learned about Robin—and her son's arrest—from us, so it had taken some consoling to calm her down first, but then she'd promised to look after Melody.

I fell asleep in the car and only woke up when Jackson pulled over. We were outside a low L-shaped concrete building in the middle of a residential neighborhood. It looked a bit like a school, only smaller, with a nicely-landscaped front yard.

"Where are we?"

"Our Lady's orphanage."

That explained the church at the end of the street, then.

"Do you think Mrs. Morgan is here?"

"I just want to ask some questions."

We were shown to the office of the Mother Superior, an honest to God—sorry—nun. I wasn't a very good Catholic, and there hadn't been any members of religious orders attending the church I'd gone to as a child, so I didn't quite know how to relate to her.

"Mrs. Morgan is a respected lay member of our orphanage," she told us with a happy smile that I thought was at odds with her black habit. "She comes over once a week and helps with the basic medical needs of the children."

"And was she here yesterday?"

"Yes. In fact, she stayed the night to take the older children to a special early-morning Mass. She sometimes does that."

That would explain why she hadn't been home.

"What age are your children?" Jackson asked, as if he hadn't registered the interesting bit, but I knew nothing went past his notice.

"Mostly three years up. When they turn eighteen we send them out into the world, and younger than three tend to be adopted fast."

"So you have an adoption service too?"

"Yes, we're a very trusted and popular service. Only the best families adopt from us. We make sure of that."

"How do your children arrive to you?" I asked.

"All sorts of ways. The parents die without anyone to take care of the children. Some are outright abandoned. Those are difficult cases, but we have excellent therapist here. And then we have the baby box."

I perked. "Baby box?"

She sighed. "For mothers to safely leave their unwanted babies to. Not everyone has access to social services or adoption advice, or they've kept the pregnancy a secret. Whatever the reason, they can anonymously and without shame leave their baby to us and we'll find them loving homes."

"How does it work?"

"It's a hatch in the orphanage wall the size of a small crib, which it in fact is. Padded and heated, and with an alarm system, so that we know the instant a baby's been left there."

I'd never heard of such a service before, but there'd seldom been unwanted pregnancies among my friends. And they probably would've used an adoption service if there were. "Is it used a lot?"

"Too much, I'm afraid. We had to close it for a while last year. There were so many babies coming in we couldn't find them good homes fast enough. But then we were asked by Social Services if we could open it again, so we did." She looked sad for all those unwanted children.

"Do you monitor the hatch with a camera?" Jackson asked.

She nodded. "We didn't use to, to protect the anonymity of the mothers. But we've had all sorts of trouble with it from people who don't like the service. They were leaving dog excrement there, and even a dead cat once, so we had to install a camera. But we only check the feed if something bad has happened," she assured us.

"Could we see the feed?"

"May I ask why?"

"Babies have been kidnapped in this area in the past couple of months. We're trying to find out where they've disappeared to."

She crossed herself, horrified. "You think they've been put into our baby box? Whatever for?"

"Has there been any unusual activity at the box lately?"

She went to shake her head and then reconsidered. "Well, there have been babies a bit older than the newborns we mostly get." Tears sprang to her eyes. "Do you think they were kidnapped? We've adopted most of them out already."

"If we could take a look at the security footage, we would know more," Jackson said calmly.

"We only keep the footage for about three months."

"That's long enough for us."

Mother Superior led us through the orphanage to a small back office that had probably been a supply closet at some point, but now served as a security room. "We have cameras monitoring the premises too," she explained, and I felt brief dismay at the world where a Catholic orphanage needed such measures. "There's usually a young man taking care of these, but he doesn't work on Sundays."

"That's okay," Jackson said. "I know this system."

She left us to it, pleading a conflict of interest. She didn't want to witness the mothers bringing their babies, in case she recognized them. I took out my notebook with the dates the babies had been taken, and Jackson opened the archived footage.

I'm not sure what I expected—or wanted—to find. On one hand, having proof that Mrs. Morgan was behind the abductions would solve our case. But on the other hand, going after a woman who helped orphans in her free time seemed cruel.

The footage was fast to go through. The system only recorded when someone approached the hatch, so there wasn't much of it. Even without the dates to guide us, we could've managed it in less than ten minutes, as the camera had recorded only fifteen times.

And on seven of those times, it was triggered by Mrs. Morgan.

"Fuck," Jackson said, with feeling.

"You didn't want it to be her either?"

"I guess not. Let's copy this for Trevor. And then we need to see the adoption records."

But the Mother Superior wasn't willing to release them without a court order. Jackson wasn't deterred. "How about I show you pictures of the abducted babies and you can tell us if they match your records?"

She agreed to that and Jackson took out his phone where he had the photos. When we were finished, the old nun was crying. "I'm so sorry. I had no idea."

"This isn't your fault. Someone simply found a way to abuse your system."

"What shall I tell the new parents of those babies?"

"We'll worry about that later. Let's concentrate on finding the person behind it first."

"It's Mrs. Morgan, isn't it? You wouldn't have asked about her otherwise."

But Jackson wouldn't say anything. We just thanked her and left. The moment we were in the car I called Trevor. "We have the evidence you need about Mrs. Morgan."

"Are you fucking kidding me? Now we only need to find her."

"She wasn't at the church?"

"She'd already left when we got there. And listen to this: a woman at the food kitchen had her baby kidnapped there today. There were police at the scene already when we arrived."

My heart sank. "She's kidnapped another baby?"

"Yes. So we have to find her before she gives it away."

"In that case, send someone to monitor the baby box at the Our Lady's orphanage."

"Is that how she delivers them? Is the orphanage involved?"

"They had no idea. I think she only wanted to make sure the babies got a better chance, and thought that would ensure it."

"Are you at the orphanage? Can you ask if there's been a baby delivered these past two hours?"

"We just left. But we checked all the footage and there was nothing today."

"Fuck. The church is right by the orphanage. Surely she would've delivered it immediately."

"Maybe she wants to hold on to it until the police go away?"

"Then where will she be in the meantime? She isn't home. I have people monitoring it."

I gave it a thought. "Have you checked at her daughter's place? She was released from the hospital today."

"Would she take the baby there?"

"I have no idea what she would do. But we'll head there now, in case Melody knows a place her mother would like to go."

"I'm right behind you." He hung up.

Jackson was usually a very good driver, following the traffic rules and never speeding, but now he practically flew through town towards Melody's apartment. The Sunday traffic was mercifully sparse, so it didn't take us long to get there. We waited for Trevor to reach us before exiting the car.

"How do you want to handle this?" Jackson asked.

"Let's keep this as a social call," he suggested.

"We left her here less than two hours ago," I said. "She's bound to be suspicious, especially if we start asking about her mother. I'm not sure she's stable enough to face the fact that her mother took Robin."

"We'll tread carefully."

We climbed to Melody's floor through the sounds of late Sunday afternoon at home—football and fighting. We reached the correct door and Trevor was about to knock when it fell open. We stiffened. I remembered the sight that had met us the previous time this had happened, and reached for my phone to call an ambulance. My brother pulled out his gun. Clearly he had a different scenario in mind.

He pushed the door open and stepped in. "Melody? This is the police. I'm coming in." There was no response, and my stomach fell. We walked deeper into the small apartment and paused.

Mrs. Paige was lying in the middle of the floor, blood pouring from her head.

Chapter Twenty-two

B Y THE TIME THE AMBULANCE ARRIVED we'd managed to revive Mrs. Paige enough for her to tell us what had happened while I pressed a towel against her temple to stem the wound there. The apartment was otherwise empty, no sign of Mrs. Morgan, Melody, or the baby.

"It was Mrs. Morgan. I don't know what got into her. She showed up here with a baby and claimed it was Robin. And when Joanna said Robin was dead and it wasn't her baby, she got furious. I tried to take the baby away from her and that's when she hit me."

"Do you have any idea where they could've gone to?" Trevor asked. He'd already issued a statewide bolo—a police lookout alert—for Mrs. Morgan and the baby, but anything that might make it faster to find them would be appreciated.

"She kept talking about how they would all go to a good place."

We exchanged grim glances. Mrs. Morgan wasn't talking about killing them all, was she?

"What would she consider a good place?" Jackson asked sensibly.

"I don't know. Anything where a baby would be happy, I guess."

"The playground?" I suggested, and we moved as one to the window to take a look across the street, but the playground was empty at this time of evening. Just in case, Trevor directed the patrols to all playgrounds nearby.

"It's been almost two hours. They could've gotten out of the state already," he noted.

I shook my head. "If Mrs. Morgan thinks the baby is Robin, she's clearly not in her right mind. She wouldn't think of escaping, because she doesn't have any reason to escape."

"You think she's heading to a familiar place?"

I shrugged. "A place that would make her happy, I guess." We turned to Mrs. Paige, but she shook her head.

"I don't know her well."

"So who does, besides Melody?" Trevor asked.

"Mom."

I had my phone out before I'd finished the thought. It took a while for her to pick up, and when she did she instantly demanded to know why we hadn't come to Sunday lunch.

"Mom, we're in the middle of something important."

"More important than your family?"

There was no right answer to that. "Today, yes. And I need your help with it."

"That's a first."

I ignored her sarcasm. "Do you know any place where Mrs. Morgan from your work would like to spend time? Where she would be really happy?" She was quiet. "And we're in quite of a hurry."

"I understand. I'm thinking. There's the church and orphanage."

"We have those covered."

"Then all I can think of is the Prospect Park Lake. She likes to go there to watch the birds on her breaks. There's this gazebo looking over to Duck Island on the southern end of the lake."

My heart skipped a beat. "I know exactly where it is. Thanks, Mom." I hung up before she could guilt me into coming home tonight. "It wasn't a coincidence Robin's body was found at the lake. It's her favorite spot."

It energized the room. "She'll take the baby there, to complete her delusion that he's still alive," Trevor said, already heading out the door, digging out his phone as he went. We made to follow, then remembered Mrs. Paige and stopped. She waved us on.

"Go. I'm all right. The ambulance will be here soon." Since we could already hear the paramedics on the stairs, we hurried after Trevor, catching him just as he reached his car, and dove in with him. No point in taking two cars, especially since his came with a removable blue light that cleared the street before us.

The mile and a half took us less than five minutes even with some traffic on Parkside Avenue. When we reached the edge of the park, Trevor cut the blue light and drove slowly and silently along the bike lane to the lake. He pulled over well out of sight of the gazebo and we exited the car.

"Let's go in casually, in case she's unstable. We don't want to scare her into doing something rash. The baby is our number one priority."

It was incredibly difficult to walk calmly and casually when I was so tense I could barely breathe. So I slipped my arm around Jackson's and leaned against him for support. He gave me a baffled glance.

"For show," I said, but in truth I could barely stand up without him there. I was cold and relied on his warmth. I had no idea what to expect, but I didn't want to witness a dead baby. Or worse, be the reason a baby died.

The sun was setting, and the gazebo and the lake behind it were cast in red and orange light. The police crime scene tape had been removed already, but I couldn't detect any movement inside the log construction. It was quiet outside too, the last joggers having headed home already and the birds having gone quiet for the night.

"Eerie," I said in low voice as we neared the gazebo. "Should we go in?"

By way of answering, Trevor walked straight in, contrary to all his training. If Mrs. Morgan was armed, he made a perfect target silhouetted against the doorway. My breathing caught and Jackson tensed against my arm too, but nothing happened, so we followed him in.

Melody was there alone, sitting on one of the benches attached to the wall, calmly breastfeeding the baby. She glanced up when she noticed us. "He was hungry and my breasts were aching with too much milk, so I thought I'd feed him." Then she returned her attention to her task. Trevor crouched in front of her, claiming her attention.

"Melody, I'm Detective Hayes. We need to find your mother. Do you know where she is?"

"She isn't herself," she said, looking sad.

"I know, that's why we need to find her."

She shook her head. "I don't understand what she was thinking, bringing this baby to me, as if he were mine, as if it would help. She didn't even want me to have Robin and wanted to take him away. She should be happy."

I felt my throat tighten with unshed tears and Trevor had to clear his too. "I think she cared more than she thought, and it affected her greatly when he died." There was no reason to tell Melody yet why her mother was so strongly affected by the death.

"Is this where they found my baby?"

"Yes."

She smiled a sad smile. "I'm glad he died in such a beautiful place."

Trevor patted her knee and got up, brushing the baby's head lightly. "Is it long since your mother left?" His voice was gruff with emotion. I could barely breathe myself for tears that were falling down my face, and Jackson tightened his hold of my arm, clearly struggling too.

"No, she went to feed the ducks."

There was no one outside, but Trevor nodded. "I'll go look for her." He indicated with his head that I should stay with Melody, and though I'd much rather have been anywhere else, I sat next to her. Trevor and Jackson left.

"Beautiful baby," I said, to break the silence.

"Yes, but he looks nothing like my Robin. Why do you think Mom would think he did?"

"Grief manifests in odd ways."

"I don't know what I should do next. It's hard to believe Robin is gone. I guess I should bury him too." Her tears began to fall.

"Have you been to see him?"

"No. Do you think I should?"

Since I hadn't managed it, I could only shrug. "I've heard it sometimes helps with coming to terms with the death. But no one's forcing you."

"Maybe I'll wait until the funeral home has prepared him."

"That's a great idea."

We sat in silence that was only broken by the occasional suckling sound from the baby. Then she asked: "Do you think it's terribly expensive, a funeral?"

"I've never had to arrange one."

"I'll manage it. I can take more shifts at work now…" She broke down, sobbing, clutching the baby so hard against her chest he began to protest. I stroked her back until she calmed down.

"Maybe you could invite Mrs. Clark to help with the funeral," I suggested, just to have something constructive to say.

"I'll think about it." She wiped her tears and lifted the baby up against her shoulder, her movements assured. "It's so weird that this isn't my baby. Do you think his mother misses him much?"

"Yes. But we'll get him back to her, don't worry."

"It was my mother who took all those other babies too, wasn't it?"

This was the conversation I hadn't wanted to have with her. "We're still investigating it."

"I know it is. Who else could've gotten into my home without me reacting? She was going to give him away, wasn't she? Her own grandchild."

"We don't know that yet. Maybe she wanted to give you a chance to sleep by bringing him here, her favorite spot." The more I thought about it, the more it made sense. Why else would she have come here? It was miles from the orphanage, in the opposite direction from Melody's home.

"And then he died."

"Yes."

We sat in silence until Trevor and Jackson returned. "We can't find her," Trevor said.

"She went to feed the ducks," Melody repeated.

"Where?"

"On Duck Island."

The men crossed the gazebo to peer through the dusk at the island across the lake. "There are no boats. How would she get there?"

But Melody just shrugged.

An hour later, the divers from the fire department found Mrs. Morgan's body in the lake. By then, Social Services had come to take the baby and Melody away, the first to return to his mother, the latter back to the hospital, "Just in case," as it was put. We remained on the scene until the coroner's van left with Mrs. Morgan's body, not speaking the whole time. When the tail-lights disappeared, Trevor wrapped his arm around me.

"Let's go home. I have a son to tuck in."

Epilogue

THE AFTERMATH TOOK DAYS. The police had to locate all the babies that had already been adopted and return them to their rightful mothers. Only one mother opted to give her consent to the adoption after seeing how nice a home her child now had. Some of the adoptive parents talked about suing, but who they would sue was unclear. Mrs. Morgan was dead, and the orphanage was an unwitting accomplice. But the police did close the baby box for now.

All this we learned from Detective Kelley, because Trevor took a week off to spend time with his son, renting a cabin upstate and leaving his work phone home. He sorely needed the break, and the chance to be a proper father. I hoped he would return rested and happy.

As for Jackson and me, it took a couple of days for things to normalize. We tried to carry on as usual with the cases we had, but I noticed that both of us paused and stared off into space more often than usual. We didn't smile much, and not even Misty's presence, or Cheryl's baking that she brought every day, helped. I couldn't say if it was Robin's death or Mrs. Morgan's that affected us most. The first was a tragedy, but the latter robbed us of closure. We would never know for sure why she'd taken all those babies.

We attended Robin's funeral on Tuesday. It was a small occasion, with only Mrs. Paige, Jackson, and I present apart from Melody, Mrs. Clark, and Steve. He looked shell-shocked, but I hardened my heart. It would be a growing experience for him.

Mrs. Clark had paid for everything, as she told me afterwards. "I'll be looking after Joanna from now on. She needs someone with her. She's a bright young woman. She just needs someone to believe in her."

I felt more hopeful for hearing it, and hoped, too, that Mrs. Clark would have a more attentive daughter in her than her son was.

We didn't attend Mrs. Morgan's funeral that was arranged by the orphanage. "She was a respected member once," Mother Superior said, looking sad. "We'll never know what made her do such horrible things, but that's no reason not to give her a decent burial."

Thom dropped by the agency to apologize for abandoning me so rudely at the party. "I didn't even make sure you got home safely."

"That's okay. Jackson was there."

"And I noticed you spent time with Jonathan too."

I blinked before I realized he meant Moreira. "Yes, he helped me to look for the thief."

"Well, that's what he does best," he assured me with a smile. I was speechless.

The detectives had no clues about the thief's identity, and the case was about to move to other people, much to their aggravation. And mine.

"I really need to find this guy," I complained to Jackson as we returned to the office from lunch on Thursday.

"It's not our case," he reminded me calmly.

"He's bested me twice. That can't go unpunished."

"Or you could think that twice is enough and let the police handle it."

I snorted. "Do you not know me at all?"

He smiled, but before he could answer Cheryl greeted us from behind her desk: "This was delivered when you were away." She held up a small packet. Jackson went to take it, but she pulled it away. "It's for Tracy."

I skipped in to claim the packet, feeling giddy. "For me? It isn't even my birthday." I shook the packet but it didn't make any sound. It was the size of my palm and weighed nothing.

"When is your birthday, anyway?" Jackson asked.

"April," I said absentmindedly, ripping open the tape on the packet. "Which you very well know, having seen my personal info when I started here."

I got the packet open, but the insides were just filling paper. I removed them to reveal a black velvet box, the kind one buys jewelry in. We all leaned closer, as if to make sure we saw correctly.

"You have a secret admirer," Cheryl said.

"Apparently."

"Well, open it."

I picked the box from the packet and opened it. Inside was a pair of gemstone earrings. Cheryl inhaled in awe, but I'd gone cold inside. I knew those earrings. They belonged to Melissa.

"There's a note in the packet," Cheryl said, picking it up. "Until we meet again. Oh, how romantic."

But Jackson and I exchanged grim looks. The thief had returned the earrings he stole. The thief knew who I was, and he was sending a message.

What the hell?

Acknowledgements

This was an easy book to write, despite the grim topic, and that doesn't happen often in an author's life. So I'd like to thank all the muses and gods of creative writing out there, whichever of you chose to help me. Keep up the good work.

I'd also like to thank my husband for his patience and my sisters for their helpful comments. And, as always, my editor, Lee Burton, for his good job. All the remaining mistakes are mine.

And you, reader, I thank you too. I wouldn't be here without you.

About the Author

Susanna Shore is an independent author of more than twenty books. She writes Two-Natured London paranormal romance series about vampires and wolf-shifters that roam London, P.I. Tracy Hayes series of a Brooklyn waitress turned private investigator, and House of Magic paranormal mysteries. She also writes stand-alone thrillers and contemporary romances. When she's not writing, she's reading or-should her husband manage to drag her outdoors-taking long walks.

You can find more about Susanna on her webpage at
www.susannashore.com

Tracy Hayes,
from P.I. with Love

THERE'S SOMETHING TO BE SAID about Christmas in New York. It's loud, colorful and bright—and it goes on for fricking ever. Even for someone who actually loves Christmas. I'd heard all my favorite Christmas tunes by the end of November, and I wasn't even that frequent a shopper. Four days before the D-day, I was heartily bored with most of them. If I had to listen to Mariah Carey bleat through 'All I Want for Christmas' one more time, I'd have to bludgeon someone to death with my beanie.

That I was forced to wear a beanie might account for some of the aggression. I wasn't a hipster enough to pull it off, and it hid my one distinguishing feature: my hair; shoulder length and fire engine red again, after a brief period of cotton candy pink. With it on, my average face would've gone unnoticed, if it weren't for the slightly frost-bitten nose and cheeks. Not that those were an improvement.

We were experiencing unseasonably cold weather that had reduced all but the most foolhardy fashionistas to becoming walking advertisements for winter clothing if we hazarded the outdoors. And occasionally indoors too, because the strain the cold put on the power grid had caused shortages, and at times we were completely without heat, like today at the office.

Jackson Dean Investigations, the private investigator firm I worked for, was located in an old but fairly nice building on Flatbush Avenue in Brooklyn, not far from the Barclays Center. The neighborhood was prosperous and the clientele that the location lured in could pay our fees. We had two rooms, a larger one facing the street that I shared with Jackson Dean, my boss, and a smaller reception area that was the dominion of Cheryl Walker, the office goddess. In general, the building management kept the place in good repair, but they hadn't anticipated this weather and the heater had broken. We were on the second day of no heat and it was freezing in there.

In addition to the tasseled woolen headgear, I was wearing a black down coat several sizes too large for me. I'd salvaged it from the closet of my brother Trevor who was quite a bit bigger than me, tall and wide-shouldered. It wasn't quite at its peak of usability anymore, but I could fit a thick sweater Mom had knitted for me underneath—plus a couple of other layers too. I wore a woolen scarf around my neck and I was holding a hot mug of coffee in my mittened hands.

Jackson was wearing a black long-sleeved T-shirt instead of his usual short-sleeved one. I swear that man had to have hot lava running in his veins to be able to sit by the windows that were covered with ice, and not freeze to death. That, or his muscles created kinetic energy even when he was seemingly in repose, keeping him warm.

They were very fine muscles, so who knows what sort of feats they were capable of.

Lately, he'd begun to hint that I should work towards similar muscles too, just so I would able to take a bad guy if the need arose. He'd even promised to buy me a membership in an inexpensive gym near his home he went to. So far, I had heroically resisted, preferring my hard-earned round parts, even if some of those stubbornly clung to my waist. It was bad enough he made me jog regularly.

When he went out, he didn't wear a hat, even though his dark brown hair was currently cut short after Cheryl made him have it tidied, and the cold had to bite. He would occasionally put on gloves, but he only remembered to close his winter parka if I or Cheryl reminded him of it. But at least he wore the coat.

Cheryl, for her part, was wearing trousers for the first time that I'd ever seen her. Pink, naturally, like pretty much everything she wore. Honest-to-god Ugg boots protected her feet, also the first time I'd ever seen her in flats. The pink angora sweater she had on today was so fluffy it practically doubled her already ample girth. Misty Morning, her Border terrier-Yorkie mix had the cutest pink down coat and boots when she went out, though she refused to wear them indoors. She was currently sleeping next to me on the couch that was my workspace, leaning against my thigh and warming it nicely.

On top of the cold spell, a snow storm of the century—because we're not at all prone to hyperbole—was predicted for the Christmas Day, sending everyone to panic and hoarding frenzy. That included my mother. Her pantry was so well-stocked by now, that the entire family, spouses and grandchildren included, would survive until Epiphany.

I wasn't panicking. Mom would feed me, and even if the storm hit earlier than predicted, paralyzing the city, I had all my Christmas preparations done. My sister Tessa and I had gone to our traditional Christmas shopping trip to Manhattan two weeks ago. I helped her select her presents and in return she paid for mine. It's not quite as exploitative on my part as you might think. Tessa is a brilliant doctor with a clinical mind, and she absolutely lacks the imagination and the initiative to buy presents. She doesn't quite understand the need for the ritual of exchanging gifts, and in her opinion, only practical gifts should be given. Since she earns well as a doctor—and doesn't have any student loans—whereas I had barely survived for years on minimum wage and tips when I was waitressing, the arrangement suited us both. I was doing better now as an apprentice P.I., but I saw no reason to alter the arrangement. I might need that money later.

The presents that I had to buy myself, for Jackson, Cheryl and Jarod, my roommate, I'd bought online well in advance. Jackson would get a T-shirt with a picture of Sherlock Holmes and a text 'On par with the best' on it. I thought it described him perfectly, plus it wouldn't put an undue strain on our boss-underling relationship. Things had been slightly weird since Thanksgiving, largely because he'd kissed me. He'd been worried to death for me, which explained it, and while it was a great kiss, I needed things to be back to normal. He hadn't even yelled at me lately—much.

Everything I'd ordered had arrived in good time, had been as advertised and were now wrapped nicely. Online shopping was so easy that I hoped Tessa would never learn about it. Not solely so that she could keep paying for my presents, but because the shopping trip was basically the only time we went anywhere as sisters and I didn't want to lose that. We seldom saw each other as it was, if you didn't count my all too frequent visits to her ER since I started as an apprentice P.I.—which, sadly, I did.

One Christmas present was yet to be bought, however: Tessa's for her live-in partner Angela. They'd been together for such a short time that I didn't know her well yet, and had no idea what she would like. Tessa, obviously, was no help. She would've wanted to buy her an espresso machine, and couldn't understand at all when I said it wasn't romantic enough.

I tried to imagine what I would want from the person I loved, but my ex-husband, in addition of being a bastard band-leader that had cheated me with a groupie, had been utterly negligent when it came to presents. I would've been happy even with the espresso machine, just as long as he would've remembered.

I was browsing websites for inspiration, but I had nothing. It was as if my brain had frozen too. I drank some coffee, but it didn't help. Angela was a pediatrician, Italian and catholic, none of which helped me to figure out what she might like from the woman she loved. Frustrated, I sighed loud enough for Jackson to give me a questioning look.

"What are you giving Emily for Christmas?" I asked, a true testament to how stuck I was.

A panicked look spread on his face. It was a manly face, clean lined with dark brown brows and eyes, and it could express a wide range of emotions from amusement to anger and then revert to almost unnoticeable. But what it never, ever expressed, was panic. He was thirty-five, eight years older than me, and a former homicide detective turned P.I. He had seen it all, and had the eyes of a seasoned cop to go with it.

Nothing ever fazed him. Except the thought of buying a Christmas present for his girlfriend.

"I don't know. Why do you ask? Could you suggest something?"

I rolled my eyes, blue and as seasoned as any Brooklyn waitress'. "If I had even inkling, I wouldn't ask you. But never mind. Cheryl!" I yelled through the open door. "What should Tessa give Angela for Christmas?"

"A locket," she immediately answered, and I perked, excited.

"Excellent idea." I instantly googled for lockets and inspiration abounded.

"Can I give Emily a locket too?" Jackson asked hopefully.

"No!" Cheryl and I answered simultaneously, and he looked hurt.

"Why not?"

How to explain? "It's a more intimate gift than what your relationship seems to be," I said, awkwardly. They'd been together for almost six months, but he'd intended to end the relationship many times already. Why he hadn't, I had no idea.

"So, no jewelry?" he asked, not terribly upset by my estimation.

"You can give her earrings," Cheryl consoled him, entering the office in her pink gorgeousness. "And I know just the place where you can get both your presents. Bundle up, and follow me."